Sammy in Holland

Single Wide Female Travels
Book 3

By

Lillianna Blake

DEDICATION

To all women out there who've been told
that they need to chill out just a bit. ☺

TABLE OF CONTENTS

CHAPTER 1

I fiddled with the corner of my ticket. With the flight delay it was a bit of a wait. Max stirred in his sleep but didn't wake up. I took a deep breath and looked down at my ticket again. I couldn't quite figure out what had me feeling so nervous.

After I'd spoken on the phone to Erik, my contact in Amsterdam, I did wonder what was in store for me. All the other stops on the book tour had been hosted by women. It wasn't as if I didn't like the idea of a man hosting me. I just wasn't sure what to expect.

The PA system came to life and announced the boarding of our flight.

"Max." I patted the top of his knee. "The plane is leaving."

"Aw, I just fell asleep."

I raised an eyebrow but decided not to point out that he'd been snoring on my shoulder for at least a half hour. He sleepily gathered our luggage. The flight itself was already scheduled to leave late, but the new delay had us arriving well after midnight.

It wasn't a very crowded flight, which gave us the opportunity to sprawl out in our seats. Max looked over at me.

"Are you ready for Amsterdam?"

"I'm looking forward to it." I smiled.

"You know, I did a little research about the place. Did you know that certain things are legal there?" He grinned.

"Oh, that kind of research." I laughed. "Yes I did know that in fact."

"So?"

"So what?" I raised an eyebrow.

"When in Amsterdam…"

"No way." I shook my head. "The only thing that would likely lead to is me getting a very bad case of the munchies. That's the last thing I need to do after our gelato tour." I laughed, but I was definitely serious about wanting more food control in my life. "I did some research too. I'm looking forward to riding bicycles everywhere. That should give me the opportunity to work some of Venice off."

"No more motorcycles?" Max pouted.

"Not this time. It'll be Sammy powered."

Max glanced away for a moment. "I'm not sure it's such a good idea. You might get too worn out."

"I don't think so." I shook my head. "I'll be fine. I'm actually dying for some physical activity."

"We walked a lot in Venice. I'm sure we could find some trails to hike in Amsterdam. Or maybe some other kind of activity."

"But biking is so much fun. Besides, that's how everyone gets around there. We won't be able to avoid it, so we might as well enjoy it."

Max glanced away.

I could almost imagine I heard him wince, and when he turned back around toward me, he was frowning.

"Okay, I guess that's what we'll do then. I'm going to get a little more sleep."

I waited for him to rest his head on my shoulder again, but instead he propped his head against the window. I opened my mouth to protest, but his eyes were already closed.

He must be more tired than I thought. I stifled a yawn, realizing that I was tired as well. I closed my eyes for what I thought was just a moment.

When I opened my eyes again, the flight crew was busy preparing for our descent. It seemed like no longer than a minute, but it must have been much longer. I looked over at Max, whose head was still propped against the window. Before I could wake him, he opened his eyes.

"Finally, we're here."

"Didn't you sleep?"

"A little."

I kissed his cheek. "I'm looking forward to exploring

Amsterdam with you."

"Me too." He grabbed our luggage from the overhead compartments and we headed off the plane.

It was easy to navigate our way through the airport, but when we reached the door it occurred to me that I had no idea whether or not Erik had sent a car for us. I also didn't have a clue or an address to where we were staying.

I checked my phone to see if I'd missed any texts or calls from him while we'd been in the air. There wasn't even an e-mail.

"We can find a taxi, I'm sure." Max held the door open for her.

"To where, though? I have no idea where we're supposed to be staying." I heard the stress in my own voice as I listened to the ringing of the call I'd made. When Erik's voicemail picked up, my heart sank. I gritted my teeth.

"Hi, Erik, this is Samantha. We're here at the airport. I'm not sure where we're supposed to be staying or how we're supposed to get there. If you can give me a call back right away that would be great." I hung up the phone and sighed. "What if he's sleeping?"

"Hey, don't worry." Max rubbed the length of my arms. "We're capable of finding our own transportation and a place to stay."

"But it shouldn't be like this. He should have someone here—the same way that all of our other hosts have had arrangements made for us. If he can't get this straight, then what will the book signing be like?"

"Well, give him another call. If he doesn't get back to us, I say we find our own way and connect with him after the sun is up."

"Okay." I dialed Erik's number again. Once more it went to voicemail. I didn't bother to leave another message. "Well, that's that. It looks like Amsterdam is going to be a flop."

"None of that, remember? We're leaving the stress behind us."

"Ugh. Max, you're so right." I planted as big kiss on his lips, then smiled. "This can be an adventure. I'll look up what nearby hotels might be good for us to stay in."

"I'll see what I can do about getting us a taxi."

A few minutes later we were on our way. Maybe my contact was sound asleep in his bed somewhere, but I looked forward to discovering Amsterdam anyway. It was nearly dawn and not yet light enough to see much of what we passed, but Amsterdam seemed to have an energy of its own—hopeful, light and full of potential.

LILLIANNA BLAKE

CHAPTER 2

The hotel was nice enough and the bed looked very appealing, but the sun was just coming up and I didn't want to waste a minute of time in Amsterdam.

"I'm starving. I wonder if they have a mini-bar." I looked around for a small refrigerator.

"None of that. I'll go downstairs and get us some breakfast. I think that little cafe we saw might be open now. Maybe some pastries?"

"Max." I met his eyes.

"Okay, okay. It'll be something healthy, I promise." He kissed me then headed right back out the door.

The moment that Max was out of the room, I felt my blood begin to boil. Sure, Max thought it was best to take the casual approach and simply accept that Erik might have forgotten us at the airport. But I couldn't. How difficult was it to arrange some transportation for us? If Erik hadn't been able to do it, he should have just let me know ahead of time so that we'd have it taken care of. Instead, our first moments in Amsterdam had been a bit stressful so far.

I sighed and sat down on the bed. As I toyed with my phone a text came through.

Did you take an earlier flight?

I stared at the text. It was clearly from Erik. Was he trying to convince me that he didn't know my flight schedule? I thought about whether to text him back or not. After a few minutes, I realized I had no choice. Eventually we'd have to deal with one another, and it would be better if there weren't any conflict.

No, we took the flight that we were given tickets for.

It was short and sweet, maybe more short than sweet, but it got the message across.

An instant later I received another text.

You couldn't have. Your flight isn't supposed to get in until three.

I rolled my eyes and fired a text back.

Three in the morning, not three in the afternoon. We found our own way from the airport. We rented a hotel room.

I waited for him to respond with an apology or something close to it. Instead, I received no response. As the minutes slipped by, I grew more aggravated. Was it not important to him that we'd had to find our own way?

Ten minutes later my phone rang. When I saw that it was Erik I picked it up.

"Hallo. I see things are off to a bumpy start. There was some confusion?"

"We weren't confused, Erik. We were at the airport, right where we were supposed to be, but I did get confused when there was no transportation waiting for us."

"We can fix that. I've rented a place that I think you're going to like. Should we meet for breakfast?"

"My husband is already out getting us breakfast at the moment. Erik, I understand if it was a mistake. I don't want us to get off on the wrong foot. Let's just talk about the book signing. Do you have it booked?"

"Yes, of course. I thought you might like to try something a little different. I'll surprise you."

"I'm not really that comfortable with surprises."

"Oh, don't worry, you're going to find that things in Amsterdam are a lot more fun than anywhere else. Meet me for lunch and we'll go over all the details."

"Okay, just send me the address."

"I'm looking forward to meeting you, Samantha."

"Me too." I hung up the phone before I could add another remark. I'd looked forward to meeting him at the airport when I'd landed too. Hopefully it wasn't a sign of missed meetings to come.

The door to the hotel room swung open and Max walked in with fruit parfaits and coffee.

"Who was that?" He glanced at my phone as I put it down on the table.

"Erik. Apparently he thought we were landing at three in the afternoon, not three in the morning."

"Hm." Max quirked a brow. "Sounds a bit unprofessional."

"I agree. Thanks for this." I kissed his cheek. "We're supposed to meet him for lunch."

"Great. I'm sure once we have the chance to talk to him we can straighten things out. Come eat." He sat down at the small table.

I joined him and inhaled the scent of the coffee.

"Oh, that is delicious."

"I have a feeling that after this tour we're never going to be satisfied with American food again." Max laughed. "I'm not sure we ever were, really."

"Hey, nothing beats a good hamburger." I took a bite of the parfait.

"Well, technically hamburgers are not an American food."

"Apple pie?"

He shook his head. "Not even close."

"Huh?" I grinned. "I never really thought about what was and wasn't. I suppose that's a good thing, though. We have a lot of variety."

"But nothing quite like this coffee." Max sighed and took a sip.

"You seem to have started a love affair with coffee on this tour."

"I have." He turned the cup slowly between his hands. "I see its power."

"Just remember, coffee is tasty, but if your body needs rest, it needs rest."

"I slept on the plane." He met my eyes.

I bit into my bottom lip. I suspected that he hadn't. It wasn't like Max to lie to me. It made my mind run wild with possible reasons, but I didn't want to dampen our first day in Amsterdam obsessing about a little white lie.

"Then we should be ready to explore, hm?" I said.

"I noticed there are a lot of walking tours. I was hoping we could take one."

"Oh, I thought the bike tours would be more fun."

"Maybe, but the walking tour lets you really take in the details, you know?"

"Sure. We can do both." I finished my parfait. "I'm really excited."

"Me too." Max looked away from me. "Did Erik text you the address?"

"I forgot all about that." I grabbed my phone and checked for a text. "No, he hasn't yet."

Erik? Where are we supposed to meet?

I waited a few minutes to see if he would return the text. When he didn't, I dialed his number.

"Voicemail again." I looked over at Max.

"He'll text us eventually. Let's head out." Max tossed the containers from our breakfast into the nearby garbage can.

"Sounds good." I walked to the door with him, but I couldn't ignore a bit of worry. Just what kind of surprise did Erik have in store for me?

LILLIANNA BLAKE

CHAPTER 3

"So very many museums." Max looked over the list of places to visit in his hand. "I'm not sure we'll have time to see them all."

"Let's just pick one for today. I'm not sure what our schedule will be like once we meet up with Erik. Oh, look at this one." I pointed to one of the museums on the list. "It has more modern and contemporary art. Maybe there will be some live exhibits."

"Live exhibits?"

"Oh yes, art as life. Haven't you ever seen one?"

"I don't think so."

"Instead of looking at a painting, the artist performs the art. Sometimes they use props or they just stage a scene. I remember hearing about a guy who stayed inside a glass box for like three days."

"What?" Max raised his eyebrows. "How is that art?"

"Well, we won't know unless we look, right?" I grabbed his hand and led him down the sidewalk.

The streets were lined with eye-catching architecture.

"I think it's this way." Max pointed to one of the

signs.

"No, it's over there." I pulled him across the street.

"Sammy, I'm telling you, it's the other way."

"Max, this is the museum." I pulled open the door for him.

He frowned and looked up and down the street. "Are you sure?"

"We're about to find out." I led him inside.

There were a few plates on display. It wasn't what I expected, but it would do. I studied the plates intently. After a few seconds, it dawned on me that these weren't just average plates. "Oh no." I turned around to face Max. "I think you were right."

His eyes were locked onto a nude painting right in front of him.

"I don't know, Sammy, this looks pretty contemporary to me. Maybe we should ask about the live art?"

"Stop it, Max. I think we're in a sex museum!"

"A what?" Max laughed. "I don't think so."

"Really?" I pointed to the portraits on the walls. Each one was as naked as the last. The images on the plates depicted some very erotic act.

"Oops." He winked at me. "You planned this, didn't you?"

"No, I did not." I laughed and pulled him away from the painting. "You are not old enough to be in here."

"I am too."

"Okay, then I'm not." I grinned as we hurried out of the museum.

Max caught me in his arms and drew me in for a kiss. It wasn't the quick peck that we'd fallen into the routine of sharing. It was a deep soulful kiss that made my knees wobble. I was startled by the flash of a camera.

"Uh, Max." I leaned close to him. "I think that we've just become the live art."

A young woman hurried past with her camera dangling from her shoulder.

"I can agree with that." Max steered me down the sidewalk. "Why don't we find the real museum we were looking for?"

"Sure."

My cell phone chimed. I pulled it out of my purse to see a text from Erik.

Where are you? Aren't we meeting for lunch?

"Can you believe this?" I read the text to Max.

He glanced at his watch. "It's only ten."

I sent a text back.

You never sent me an address. Where are you?

I tried to keep my temper in check. A few deep calming breaths did a little to help, but my nerves crackled.

Erik's next text to me contained the address—no explanation, no other direction—just the address.

I sighed and shook my head. "I guess we'll have to go meet him. I have no idea when my book signing is supposed to be."

"It's alright. We can go to the museum later." Max rubbed my shoulders. "Try not to let it get under your skin."

I relaxed. A little. After entering the address in my map app, we headed in the direction of the restaurant. It wasn't too far. I pointed out a few things to Max as I passed them by.

"Oh look, just what we talked about on the plane." He smiled and pointed to a very festive sign.

"Don't even think about it." I rolled my eyes. "The last thing I need is more reason to trip over things."

"Maybe so, but it could be fun—if you wanted to give it a try, I mean."

"You first." I smirked at him.

"Nah, I'm a bit old for that." He looked into my eyes. "Besides, I'm already high on life. How could I not be—with you in it?"

"Aw." I kissed his cheek. "So you're comparing our relationship to being half-baked?"

"Uh. That's not exactly what I meant." He laughed.

"Here it is." I pointed to the restaurant across the street. We waited for a few bicycle riders to pass, then crossed.

On the other side I noticed an assortment of flowers at a stand. "Aren't they beautiful? Look how many different colors there are."

"Just like the buildings around here."

"Yes, I do like how creative and colorful everything feels. I might just have to do some writing tonight."

"That's great. I know you didn't have much time to write in Venice."

"Honestly, I'm not sure what Erik's plans are for our visit here yet. I do hope we'll have at least a little free time."

LILLIANNA BLAKE

CHAPTER 4

As I opened the door to the restaurant, I realized that I had no idea what Erik looked like. I surveyed the people seated at tables. Most were not alone. Had Erik brought someone with him? It was possible. The only person I saw sitting alone was far too young to be Erik. He looked like he was barely twenty. Surely, that wouldn't be the person in charge of the book signing.

"Let's get a table." I slid my hand into Max's.

As the waitress approached, the young man stood up and waved to me.

"Samantha?" He smiled.

My heart sank. I looked over at Max. He raised an eyebrow at me. With reluctance I walked over to the table, Max trailing behind me.

"Erik?" I paused beside the table.

"Yes, it's me." He grinned. "I'm so glad that you're here. Please, sit."

Max pulled out a chair for me.

I sat down, with my gaze still locked onto Erik. Maybe he just looked young. Maybe he was much older.

"It's good to meet you, Erik."

Max sat down beside me.

"I've been looking forward to hearing about what you might have in store for me."

"Well, there's the signing tonight."

"Tonight?" My eyes widened. "When?"

"At five." He lifted an eyebrow. "Didn't you get my e-mail?"

"No, Erik, I didn't get an e-mail from you." I frowned. "I had no idea that you'd planned a signing for tonight."

"Oh, well, it'll be fine. Just a meet and greet sorta thing."

"No reading?"

"I guess if you want to do one." He shrugged.

I sat back in my chair and looked over at Max.

Max grimaced and lifted one shoulder.

When I looked back at Erik his attention remained on the straw in his glass of soda.

"So how are you enjoying Amsterdam so far?"

"Erik, what about the plan for while I'm in Amsterdam?"

"Oh, right. Uh, so there's the one tonight. Then tomorrow you have the day free. Then the next day I've set up something special for you."

"What?" I smiled a little.

"You'll see." He winked at me.

"Is it a signing?"

"Sort of." He fiddled with his straw.

Every little motion he made set my nerves more and more on edge. It seemed to me that his intention was to keep me guessing.

"Erik, I appreciate the effort to surprise me, but I really don't feel comfortable not knowing what is going to happen next. I'm sure that you can appreciate that."

"I can—but it is a little shocking." He met my eyes across the table.

"Why?" My eyes widened.

The waitress interrupted to take our orders. Once she'd finished, I looked back at Erik again.

"What could be surprising about wanting to have an idea about our plans?"

"It's just that every person I've spoken to has claimed that you're so easy to work with. I thought you would be more mellow, I guess."

The legs of Max's chair scraped across the floor as he changed position. I glanced over at him to see that his jaw was clenched.

"I don't mean to be difficult. It's just that without some idea of what we're doing, I'm a little anxious about what might come next. I'd rather have an idea so that Max and I can make some plans too."

"Okay, okay. Calm down." He sighed.

"What? I am calm." I narrowed my eyes. "Why would you say that I'm not calm?"

Max set a hand on my shoulder. Only then did I

realize that my heart was racing. Was Erik right? Was I being too demanding?

"The signing tonight will just be an intimate group of your biggest fans. Then tomorrow you'll be free to enjoy yourself. I would highly suggest that you imbibe of some local customs—if you know what I mean." He wiggled his eyebrows.

"No, thank you. I'm not really interested in that."

"I can tell." He laughed a little and nodded at Max, as if Max would agree with him.

Max didn't say a word.

"Actually, we were interested in seeing the Stedelijk museum, but we got a little turned around today." I frowned. I tried to keep my voice casual, but the more I tried the more uptight I felt. "And maybe a bicycle tour."

"Oh yes, you have to do that." Erik nodded. "They're great."

"I was thinking about one of the walking tours." Max cleared his throat.

"Oh no, you don't want to do that—so slow and boring. Trust me, you'll be wanting to jump into one of the canals before you're halfway through the tour."

"See?" I smiled at Max. "A bicycle tour will be a lot more fun."

Max nodded.

"The nightlife here is really fantastic. After the signing tonight, I'm going to take the two of you out." He held his hand up in the air before I could speak. "I'm not taking no for an answer. Put on something sexy, and don't expect to be home before four."

"Four?" I raised an eyebrow. "I think that's a bit late for us."

"Trust me, I'll show you a good time." He glanced at his watch. "So, there's a few hours before the signing. I should probably show you where you'll be staying."

"I think we'll be fine where we are. We don't need to move to someplace else. The hotel is quite nice."

"Nonsense! I arranged for you to have an experience, not just a place to stay. You're going to love it."

Think positive, Sammy. Don't anticipate the worst. It could be great. I smiled as I attempted to convince myself.

LILLIANNA BLAKE

CHAPTER 5

When we left the restaurant, Erik walked a few blocks with us to a strange section of housing.

"Here we are." He gestured to a ground floor section of the building that was long and narrow.

"It looks like a shipping container." Max raised an eyebrow.

"It is." Erik grinned. "Isn't it great? I knew you'd love it. They're all the rage right now—less electricity, less of a footprint, yet you still get all the things you need."

"Oh." I looked at the tiny door and the narrow walls. "So we each get one?"

"Don't be silly. A husband and wife shouldn't stay apart. Here, let me show you inside." He unlocked the door. "Single file please."

As if we had any other choice.

The interior was occupied on one side by a couch and a bed and on the other by a small sink and table, which left only a few feet of space to walk through.

"It's quaint." I swallowed hard.

"It's unique." Max looked over at me.

"It's self sustaining."

"Is there a bathroom?" I looked around but didn't see any other door.

"Ah, bathrooms can be a bit tricky. So there is a public restroom available a few feet away from the building. I'm sure you'll find it's very convenient. There's also a shower."

"I don't think that's going to work." Max crossed his arms. "We'll just stay at the hotel."

"Oh really? That's a shame. I thought for sure you'd like this." Erik turned around to face me. "I guess you're used to the luxuries of life."

My eyes widened at his words. "I wouldn't say that. But I think a bathroom would be nice."

"You'd be surprised how liberating it is to find comfort in such a small space."

I hesitated. It would be a new experience. New experiences were always something that I liked to try. It could lead to an interesting blog post.

"Why don't we try it, Max? It can't be that bad."

"Did you hear what he said about the bathroom?" Max cringed.

"I did, but I think it's worth a try. It'll certainly give us some togetherness time. Hm?" I grinned.

"I can't complain about that, I guess." Max smiled at me.

"Okay, I'll arrange for someone to bring your things over here." Erik began to tap on the screen of his cell phone.

"And put them where?" Max laughed.

"Oh, here's the closet." Erik opened the small cabinet under the sink. "Plenty of room in there for a few things."

"Very few." Max stretched his arms above his head. Thunks filled the small space as his knuckles hit the ceiling. "Ouch."

"Aw, poor thing." I grabbed his hands and kissed his knuckles. "We'll give it a shot, and if it doesn't work out, we can always go back to the hotel."

"But first let's hit one of my favorite places," said Erik.

"Somewhere we can stretch out?" Max winked at me.

"Oh yes, a great place to expand your consciousness." Erik winked at me.

I knew why Max had winked at me; I wasn't quite sure what Erik's wink meant.

I didn't have long to wonder before he ferried us to a nearby coffee shop.

"Great, I could really use some coffee."

Erik laughed as he opened the door. "Yes, right—coffee. That's it."

I looked over at Max with a raised eyebrow.

Max only shrugged. "I have a feeling this is his ride and we're just along for it."

The interior of the coffee shop was rather dim with some glowing lights scattered throughout. I thought maybe it was one of those coffee shops where people read poetry.

At the coffee bar Erik leaned forward and smiled at the woman behind the counter. "Could I have a menu, please?"

"Coming right up." She reached behind the bar and pulled out a long glossy menu.

As I looked around the coffee shop I noticed that there were quite a few people seated at the tables. Little clouds of smoke were puffing into the air all around them. As the scent met my nostrils it dawned on me that this coffee shop wasn't just for drinking coffee.

I grabbed Max's arm. "Max, this is not a normal coffee shop."

"Not at all." Max sniffed the air. "Do you want to leave?"

"I don't want to be rude."

"I don't want you to be uncomfortable."

I sighed and turned back to face Erik. When I did, I stared straight at three joints he held up in front of me.

"One for each of us—a welcome present." He held one out to me.

I had flashbacks of a friend's basement and the absolute worst music I'd ever listened to. There may have also been a strobe light involved.

"No, thank you." I stepped back some.

"No?" He laughed. "I thought you would be excited. This is what most people enjoy about Amsterdam."

"She's not interested." Max eyed him for a moment.

"You must be, though." Erik held out one of the joints to him.

"No, I'd rather not." Max smiled a little. "It's just not my thing."

"Okay." He shrugged. "More for me I suppose. What about an edible?" He gestured to an assortment of pastries, cookies, and brownies on display.

"Oh, that brownie looks good." I reached for it, but Max caught my hand.

"I thought we were eating healthier in Amsterdam?" He met my eyes.

"It's one brownie."

"It's one *special* brownie." Max quirked an eyebrow.

"Oh." My eyes widened. "I didn't realize that."

"Just about everything in here is designed to mellow you out. I'm sorry. I didn't realize that neither of you would enjoy that. We can go."

"No, it's fine. You should be able to enjoy yourself. You stay, we'll go." I smiled at him. "I don't want to be a buzz kill."

"I'll meet you at the book signing just before five." He handed me a piece of paper. "Here's a map with the location. It's only a few blocks from where you're staying." He sent a wink in my direction. "After the reading, I can introduce you to Amsterdam after dark. That, I know you're going to like."

I didn't have the heart to tell him that I likely might

not, in fact, like his version of Amsterdam after dark. I didn't want to ruin all of his fun.

"We'll be there." I hooked my arm through Max's and we left the coffee shop.

CHAPTER 6

"Well, that was interesting." Max grinned. "I think we might now know why Erik is a little forgetful."

"Yeah. I guess I should give him some credit for trying so hard to show us a good time. If we get through the book signing and survive tonight, it sounds like we'll have all of tomorrow free. I'm thinking a bike tour, the museum...maybe hit a market for some fresh fruits and vegetables."

Max nodded as he looked at me. "Sounds good. Are you ready for the book signing?"

"It's actually a little liberating that I get to decide the flow of it. I didn't expect that, but I am looking forward to it." I smiled. "The important thing is that we find a way to enjoy ourselves—no matter what."

"I like that positive attitude. I hope that it's still around in the middle of the night when you have to pee."

I cringed at the thought. "Okay, so no drinks after ten." I laughed.

"That just might work." Max grinned.

The tiny space of our temporary home didn't provide a lot of options when it came to needing a little space to move around.

"Max, I have to get changed."

"Okay." He sat down on the couch. "Do you want me to help you pick something out?"

"No. I just—" I cleared my throat and shifted from one foot to the other. "There's just not a lot of room."

"There's enough room for you to change."

"I know. You're right." I looked over at him.

He looked back at me.

In his defense there weren't many other places for him to look.

Max didn't ever do anything but compliment me. He'd shown me time and time again how much he adored my body, but in that moment, I couldn't deny the flutter in my stomach and the heat in my cheeks. I didn't want to change in front of him. It wasn't as if I'd never done so before. But something about the close quarters and my ever-changing body made me want to hide myself from him.

In an effort to be modest, I tried to change my bra under my shirt. As I wriggled around inside of my shirt I was too distracted to think about the tight space. My hip hit the table, and my knee hit the edge of the bed. I lost my balance with my arms still tangled inside my shirt. I let out a muffled cry as I started to fall, landing right in Max's lap.

He tried to hide his laughter but I could feel his whole body tremble with the force of it.

"It's not funny!"

"You should see it from out here. It's very funny." Max laughed out loud as he helped me untangle the shirt from my arms.

When I emerged from my cotton prison he looked into my eyes with such affection that I couldn't be mad at him for laughing.

"Thanks for the help."

"How did you manage to get so tied up?" He rubbed my arm where the rolled-up shirt had left a red mark.

"I guess I was trying to be a little modest."

"Modest?" He tightened his lashes. "With me?"

"I know that I've gained a bit of weight and—"

"Seriously?" He grabbed my hips before I could climb out of his lap. "Wait a minute—no running off. It's not like there's anywhere you can go."

"Max, I know it's silly. I'm sorry. It just feels strange in this tiny place, like I might as well be giving you a lap dance."

"Is that an offer?" He kissed my cheek.

"Stop it. I have a book signing to get to." I stood up from his lap, but almost wobbled right back down into it.

Max caught my back and gave me a gentle push to keep me on my feet.

"I know you do, but I don't like that you're nervous

about changing in front of me. We're way past that, right?"

"It really isn't you as much as it is this place. I feel like I'm on display, like I'm the biggest thing in the room."

"Would it make you more comfortable if I went outside?"

"Maybe." I cringed.

"Okay. I need to hunt down the bathroom anyway."

"Let me know how it is."

"If I make it back." He wiggled his eyebrows.

"Be brave, Max, be brave." I laughed as he left.

Once I was alone, I was able to get dressed a little more carefully.

So far my time in Amsterdam had served to illustrate just how uptight I was. I hoped that the book signing would give me a break from that. The moment I even thought about it, anxiety stirred within me, though. I had no idea what I'd be walking into.

A handful of fans? A roomful? Would Erik be as quirky and unreliable at the book signing as he'd been since my arrival to Amsterdam? I thought about the joints he'd taken for himself. Maybe in Amsterdam things were more relaxed—maybe it was judgmental of me to even think it—but I wasn't sure if I could tolerate him being high at the book signing.

When Max returned I met him at the door. "How was it?"

"Actually, it was far more enjoyable than I expected.

It's quite clean—now, anyway—who knows if that will continue as the evening goes on?"

"We can hope." I smiled and touched his cheek. "You know how much I love you, don't you?"

"Yes." He smiled and gazed back into my eyes. "Almost as much as I love you."

"I'm so glad that you're here with me, Max—and that we get to experience all these things together."

"Me too. Now let's go experience this mellow book signing." He grinned.

LILLIANNA BLAKE

CHAPTER 7

The building that we arrived at was much bigger than I expected. When we walked in, we were directed to a smaller room within the building. I pushed open the door and found a room filled with beanbag chairs. I stared at the colorful lumps on the floor.

"What is this? We must be in the wrong room."

"I'm glad you're here. I was running late." Erik's voice drifted from behind me.

I turned to face him. "Yes, we're here, but we're obviously in the wrong room."

"No. No, this is the right room. Isn't it great? Everyone will be so comfortable." Erik patted my shoulder. "There's a big purple one up front for you. I thought you'd appreciate a little luxury."

"I would appreciate a chair—or at least a podium." I frowned.

"I'm sorry, was this a little too outside of the box for you?"

"I wouldn't say that, it's just not what I expected. What if our guests aren't comfortable?"

"There will be some folding chairs available in case anyone has difficulty. But I thought this would make the reading a bit more intimate." He paused and pulled a remote out of his pocket. "And look at this." He clicked a button on the remote. All the overhead lights in the room switched off and pulsating lights came to life. The slow pulsation of the colored light reminded me of a horror movie.

"No, no—absolutely not." I shook my head. "This isn't going to work, Erik."

"You haven't even given it a chance."

"Because I know that this isn't going to work for me. How will I ever be able to read anything with this going on? There's not enough light."

"Oh, so you do plan to do a reading?"

"I do one at every book signing."

"But that's just the thing, Samantha. This isn't every book signing. This one is supposed to be different."

"My fans are coming here to see me because they expect a book signing—along with everything that comes with that." I crossed my arms. "Erik, I really don't mean to be difficult. I just don't think that this is going to work. Maybe it's just a little too different."

"If you give me a chance to explain, I think you might like it. There's a microphone next to your beanbag. You can speak into it, and your voice will trigger vibrations in the beanbags of each of the people attending. It will be an amazing unification of everyone here."

"Or everyone might be scared off by how strange it is." I sighed. I was ready to walk out the door and cancel the entire book signing, but it occurred to me that there had been many things in my life lately that I'd thought were odd at first. Once I'd experienced them, I'd been glad that I hadn't missed out. Maybe this was another experience that I needed to allow to happen.

"Samantha, please—just let me work my magic. If you trust me a little bit, I might be able to create something amazing."

I met his eyes. Then I looked over at Max. Max nodded his head.

"Alright, I'll give it a shot. But there's no way I can do a reading in the dark."

"Isn't that the point? They don't want to hear you read from a book, they want to hear you speak from your heart."

I considered Erik's words. I did like the idea of creating a connection with my fans that might be unique and memorable for them.

"Well then, let's see how it goes. Can you show me how the microphone works?"

"Yes. Come right over here." He pointed out a microphone tucked in beside the beanbag.

As he was showing me how to turn it on and off, a few guests entered the room. My stomach churned. What would they think? I was all about going with the flow, but to me, there was a big difference between being laid back and risking my career.

"Hello, welcome." I smiled at them. "Please make yourselves comfortable."

Our guests seemed to be giving one another some looks, but I didn't hear anyone complaining. They settled into their beanbag chairs.

As more people entered the room, I realized that maybe I was too quick to judge. No one turned around and walked out. No one demanded a chair. It seemed that my fans were much more flexible about things than I was.

I sighed and looked over at Max. He stood near the door and gave me two thumbs up. I smiled back at him, then I tried to sit down on the beanbag. It was far lower than what I was expecting.

Instead of sitting, I mostly fell into the beanbag chair. When my bottom struck the fluffy material with a thud, a bit of wind escaped me. It would have been largely ignored, if it weren't for the microphone positioned right beside the beanbag chair.

As my cheeks burned hot, everyone turned to look at me. Erik stifled a laugh.

"Uh, sorry, that was just some kind of audio problem. Erik, can you please check on that? What an awful sound." I laughed.

Other people in the audience laughed too, though I wasn't sure if it was because they believed me or because they didn't.

I fumbled with the microphone in an attempt to make

sure that it was off.

LILLIANNA BLAKE

CHAPTER 8

Once I was settled, I looked back out at my audience. Or at least I tried to. The lights were so dim that I couldn't quite make out their faces. In an odd way, it seemed to relax me. After introducing myself and chatting a bit about my book, I thought I would take the opportunity that the lighting and mood provided and share something personal of myself.

"Many times people ask me how I was able to get over my fear of success and actually put my writing out there. There were a lot of different things that went into this, but one of the most important for me was meditation. Now I know some people will say that it's impossible for them to meditate—I believed that at first myself. But with the right setting, a good dose of comfort, and a guided meditation, I believe that anyone can do it. So tonight I'd like to try that with you—just a short five-minute meditation, since we're all in a comfortable space and the setting is perfect for it. What do you think?"

Most of the audience clapped. Those that didn't nodded their heads. I spotted Erik a few beanbags away.

He looked eager to participate as he shifted into a more comfortable position. I was sure that if I used a calm soothing voice, I could guide most of the group before me into at least a few moments of meditation.

Since it was quiet in the room, I didn't see the need for the microphone. I began to walk my guests through a meditation. I described the relaxation of each muscle, the release of burdens that might be weighing the mind.

"You are in a safe, calm place. Now, there is a glow. It's not too bright and not too dim. It draws you toward it. The closer you get to that glow, the more joyful you become. The glow becomes a little brighter. You can feel it now, along your skin—like the sun on a summer day. Then it seeps through your pores. It fills your body with a deep sense of peace and love for who you are."

I moved to speak again but a loud snore interrupted me. I searched through the audience and saw that it was Erik. He snored again, even louder. There was no way that the people I'd lulled into a relaxed state could hear me over the racket. I sighed and grabbed the microphone. I would just speak quietly into it, so as not to startle them.

"As that warmth flows through you, everything feels light." My voice carried through the quiet space and soared right over Erik's snores.

Instead of deeper relaxation people began to gasp and jump up out of their beanbag chairs. A few people stumbled over each other. Two or three screamed.

"What's wrong? What is it?"

I jumped up as the rest of the people leaped out of their chairs. The only one who remained seated was Erik, still sound asleep.

"There's something in the beanbags!" someone cried out.

"Is it bugs?"

"I don't see any bugs."

"Is it some kind of earthquake?"

As the cries filled the room, I vaguely remembered Erik telling me something about the microphone being set up to send vibrations to the beanbag chairs.

"Oh no, it's okay, everyone. I'm so sorry." I groaned and looked over at Max.

He fumbled for a light switch in order to prevent panic. When he found one, instead of the room being flooded with a little light, the brightest lights I'd ever seen turned on. People, who only moments before had been in a dimly lit room, relaxed in meditation, were now being completely blinded by the intensity of the light.

"Ugh! Turn that off!"

"My eyes!"

"Who does this?"

I bit into my bottom lip as I heard more comments from others in the crowd.

Erik stood up and rubbed his eyes. "What is going on? Who turned on the lights?"

I glared at him as I dropped the microphone on the floor. "You did this."

"Did what?" He looked around at the frazzled audience. "What happened? I was deep in that meditation."

"No! You were snoring!"

"Oh, sorry." He frowned. "I might have had a bit too much to eat before coming here."

"The munchies?"

He grinned. "Relax, Sammy, everything is fine."

"No it's not fine, Erik. This is a disaster! People might even sue!"

"Trust me, they won't. Watch this." He picked up the microphone. "Hey, everyone, sorry about the technical issues. Before we start the signing, please feel free to partake of the assortment of snack foods set up in the lobby."

The moment he spoke about snacks, everyone began to move toward the lobby.

"Wow. They're hungry."

Erik winked at me. "They're mellow."

"Oh, great." I sighed. "So not only did I ruin their meditation, I probably ruined their buzz."

"No, you just enhanced it. Everyone will be fine."

"This is why I like things to be under control. When they're not, things like this happen."

"Did anything so bad happen, really?" He shrugged.

Max walked over to me and wrapped his arm around my shoulders. "You doing okay?"

"I don't know. Do you think people will be back to

get their book signed?"

"Sure they will."

"See?" Erik looked from me to Max, then back again. "Everything's fine, just relax."

I took a deep breath. I tried to be calm. But I just couldn't. The way Erik looked at me with such offhandedness made my blood boil.

"No, it's not fine! Everything is not fine!" I balled my hands into fists at my sides. "This has been one problem after another. Not only did you leave us stranded at the airport, you have us crammed into a shoebox, and then you can't even be bothered to make an actual plan for the book signing. There is no chance of any of this being successful if you don't make some kind of effort."

Erik's eyes widened. "But I made plenty of effort. I made sure you got here, I made sure that the event would be eventful. Did you ever think that maybe you expect too much from other people?"

"In this case, I don't think I expected enough."

"I'm sorry if that's how you really feel. Here in Amsterdam, we like to go with the flow of things. It's not always about what we will make happen, but what happens naturally."

"I know all about what happens naturally. In fact, my entire audience does too, since it was broadcast over the microphone." I sighed. "Can't you see that a little bit of planning would have changed this entire experience?'

"Maybe. But it wouldn't have been real. It would have

been rehearsed. Now look." Erik pointed to the people who were filing back into the room to get in line for the book signing. "You haven't lost a single fan."

I pursed my lips. I didn't want to agree with him.

CHAPTER 9

If anything, I thought my fans looked a bit more eager than they'd been when they'd first arrived. I walked over to greet them.

Instead of demanding that Erik bring me a chair and a table, I settled back into the large beanbag chair. This allowed people to sit down in front of me as I signed their books. It gave me direct eye contact and a sense of equality with the person who sat across from me.

As I looked into the eyes of each woman requesting my signature, I didn't see judgment. I saw acceptance. If they were willing to accept how the evening had gone, maybe I needed to as well.

When the book signing ended, I walked back over to Max and Erik.

"Okay, all's well that ends well, right?" I smiled at them both. "Although I do hope that the next book signing will go a bit smoother than this one."

"We can hope." Erik grinned. "So are you ready to party?"

"Party?" I raised an eyebrow.

"I'm showing you the nightlife tonight, remember?"

"Oh." I stared at him.

What would it be like to be escorted around the clubs by someone like Erik? Would he abandon us when he felt the whim? Still, I was starting to fear that I'd already spent too much of my time in Amsterdam being as uptight as Erik claimed that I was.

"Okay, absolutely. I should probably change, though. This isn't exactly a dancing outfit."

"Great idea. I wasn't going to say anything, but you really need to relax and show some skin."

Max looked over at him. "I think she's beautiful in whatever she's wearing."

"Oh sure, right. I don't disagree. But you know, this is Amsterdam nightlife. This is epic. You want to dress for it."

"How about me?" Max looked down at his slacks and button-down shirt.

"Sorry, bud, no one cares what the men are wearing." Erik laughed.

Max shook his head and smiled at me. "Want me to come back with you?"

"No, it's fine. I can meet you two at the club. Or are we going to eat first?" I looked between Max and Erik.

Max's eyes narrowed. I assumed that he'd guessed that I wanted him to entertain Erik for a little while so I could cool off.

"I know a place. I'll text you," said Erik.

"Sure." I met his eyes. "You do that."

"I will. I promise." He laughed again.

I did have to admit that, despite his reckless lifestyle, Erik was probably one of the happiest people I'd ever met.

"Okay, I'll see you two there."

As I turned to walk away, Max caught me by the elbow. "Are you sure that you want to go by yourself?"

"I'll be fine." I smiled at him and kissed him goodbye.

As I walked back toward the container that we were calling our temporary home, I tried to release all the tension from my body. It seemed to build and build whenever I wasn't in control—just little things could get out of hand, and I wouldn't realize how tense I was until it was far too late.

I tried to let go of the memory of the failed meditation and the unexpected eruption. I wanted to be free and loose, like Erik. I wanted to truly experience Amsterdam for what it was.

I was almost to the door of the container when I heard a voice behind me.

"It's you, isn't it?"

I turned to see a tall, lanky man right behind me. "I'm sorry?"

"Samantha?"

I stared at him. Was it possible that I could run into someone I knew all the way over in Amsterdam? I couldn't place his face or his voice.

"Yes, I'm Samantha. Have we met before?"

"Oh, not technically." He laughed. "I'm just one of your biggest fans."

"You weren't at the book signing tonight." I studied him closely. It was a bit unusual for a man to proclaim himself as one of my biggest fans.

"I know. I didn't get there in time." He frowned. "I'm going to the next one. I'm sorry. I probably shouldn't have approached you, but I saw you walking here, and I just couldn't resist. I hope you don't mind."

"It's fine." All of the muscles I'd relaxed grew tense again. It wasn't that I didn't trust him, but after all, I was alone in the dark in a city I didn't know with a man I'd never met before.

"What did you say your name was?"

"Cory. I've been following your book tour."

"Since I've been in Amsterdam?"

"No, since it launched." He blushed. "Desperate, I know. It's just that your book spoke volumes to me."

"My book?"

Cory nodded. "I'm sure you wrote it more for the female population, but I'm one of those rare men that is very in touch with his emotions. I find your writing to be so powerful. I just…" He looked into my eyes. "I had to meet you."

My skin crawled with discomfort. He was polite enough, but the intense way he was looking at me made me tremble on the inside.

"It was nice to meet you Cory. Would you like me to sign something for you?" I reached into my purse to find a pen.

"Oh no, I left everything back at my hotel." He frowned and then met my eyes again. "Would you be willing to do something a little strange for me?"

"What?" I eyed him with reluctance.

"I don't have anything for you to sign, but I would love it if you would be willing to sign my chest—right above my heart." He lifted his shirt up to reveal smooth skin.

I took a step back. "Maybe I could just sign the shirt."

"This shirt is garbage. I just picked it up at a discount store. Please? Just a quick little swipe of the pen, that's all I'm asking. Then I'll leave you alone and do nothing but rave about you to everyone I speak to. It would be such an amazing story to tell."

I couldn't believe it, but I was actually considering it. What harm could it do? Erik wouldn't have thought twice about it. So why was I? I uncapped the marker.

"This is permanent, you know. It may take a while to wash off."

"Oh, I'm counting on it." He smiled and held up his shirt for me.

It was odd to run the tip of the pen across his skin. It glided easily, but the thought of writing on skin was strange. It was a little bit fun too, like when I would draw on the walls of my room as a kid. I knew then that it wasn't the best place for art, but that just added to the thrill.

"There you go." I smiled as he slid his shirt back down.

"Thanks, you've really made my day. I'll be at the next signing."

"I look forward to seeing you there." I waved to him and walked the short distance to the container.

CHAPTER 10

When I unlocked the door to our container room, I found myself happy to be greeted by the cheerful interior. It hadn't actually taken long for the space—or lack of space—to grow on me. There was a lot to be said for valuing every square inch. It made me think about all of the extra space I'd had in most of the places I'd lived. Maybe I could pull off living in such a tiny place if I opened my mind to it.

I dug through my suitcase for something that would be acceptable at a club. I tugged out a loose knee-length cotton dress. It would be easy to dance in. I lifted it up to look it over, but the hem of it seemed to have caught in the zipper of my suitcase.

I tugged a little to get it free. It didn't budge. I fiddled with the zipper in an attempt to loosen the material from where it was jammed. It still didn't move. Annoyed, I pulled harder at the hem. Even if it tore I could always hem it. No matter how hard I pulled, the material would not come free. With another hard pull, the material finally gave.

As the material gave, so did my balance. I stumbled backward with the dress wound around my hands. I couldn't even reach out to catch myself. I tumbled back against the sink and hit the faucet with my elbow. The cold water began to spray out of the faucet and unto my back.

"Oh that's cold! Way too cold!"

I jumped away from the faucet and tried to straighten up but my foot caught on the small table and I tilted off to the right. When I landed, it was across the small couch. My chin hit one end and my shins hit the other. I squirmed and gulped back a scream. In the process, I rolled right off the couch and into the small shelf beside it. All of the books on the small shelf tumbled off and piled on top of me.

At least I was now on the floor. At least I couldn't fall any more. At least, that's what I thought.

I started to sit up but my hand slid through the puddle that had formed from the water on my shirt and I fell once more.

As I stared up at the ceiling of my tiny temporary home, it occurred to me that it was not designed for anyone but tiny people. I could barely walk two steps without finding something to trip over.

I sighed and closed my eyes. If I couldn't find a way to remain calm, then I'd have to try to force it.

Deep breaths. Clear mind. Don't think about the pain

in my shins or the ruined blouse on my back. When I was sure that I could handle it, I carefully got to my feet. To my surprise, the dress in my hand was not ruined. It looked just fine. One glance in the mirror, however, revealed that I was not looking fine. My hair was a mess.

I changed into the dress, then took some time to straighten out my hair.

The tiny house was meant to be an experience, not just a place to stay, but it was clear to me that it was not an experience I was really enjoying—just like the unpredictable book signing wasn't an experience that I wanted to have either. I was more determined then ever to speak to Erik about it.

I did my best to clean up the water that had spilled on the floor, and then headed out. Just outside the door, my cell phone began to ring.

"I'm on my way, Max."

"I just wanted to make sure that Erik had sent you the address."

"I honestly have no idea if he did. I haven't had a chance to check."

"Is everything okay?"

"Yes, I think so."

"Do you want me to come get you?"

"No, I can get there myself."

"Okay. I'll text you the address. Get here fast, okay? I think Erik has told me every childhood memory he's ever had."

"Aw, poor Max."

"Yes, yes—very poor." He sighed.

"I'll be there soon." I smiled as I hung up the phone.

Max always had difficulty with talkers. Although he was social, he preferred not to talk unless he had something to talk about.

A moment later my cell phone buzzed with a text from Max with the address of the restaurant.

As I headed toward it I tried not to giggle at Max's predicament. I hoped that Erik would be serious enough and willing to discuss the plans for the next book signing with me.

CHAPTER 11

When I reached the restaurant I was impressed by how small it was. The front was decorated with an assortment of stones—all different shapes, sizes, and colors. I could appreciate the artistry that went into creating something like that. It was a beautiful sight.

I opened the door and peeked inside. The interior was dim, which seemed to be something that Erik preferred. Small high round tables were scattered across the restaurant. Max and Erik sat at one of those tables.

Max's eyes lit up the moment he saw me.

"Sammy, hey—over here!"

I walked over to him and caught the tail end of Erik's description of a swimming hole he'd enjoyed in the nude.

"Weren't you cold?" I laughed as I gave Max a kiss on the cheek.

"I don't think I could ever be described as cold. I'm always moving, so I guess that keeps me warm."

"It's admirable that you can move so much. Just getting changed now was quite an exhausting effort for me." I silently berated myself for even bringing it up in front of Erik.

"Is that why you have a red mark on your chin?" Max touched the mark with a fingertip. "What happened?"

"I'd rather not discuss it." I grimaced.

"Oh, don't worry. I'll have the privilege of seeing it. Each of the containers is equipped with a video camera—for safety." Erik shrugged.

I stared at him. Were privacy laws different in Amsterdam? I really had no idea. The thought of Erik seeing me wrestle with my dress—and really anything that had happened in our container—horrified me. "You're not serious?"

"No, I'm not." He laughed. "Sorry—bad joke, bad joke." He shook his head.

"Terrible joke." I pursed my lips and looked across the table at Max. "Can you believe this guy?"

"I am learning quite a bit about him." Max grinned.

"Alright, that was in poor taste, but the look on your face was absolutely priceless." Erik smiled and gestured for the waitress to walk over. "It's my treat tonight, so please order anything you like."

I looked over the menu, curious to read the selections. There was a wide variety of food. With the clubs looming ahead of me, I thought it might be best to choose something light. I ordered a salad with chicken, feeling content with my decision.

"Salad? It's always a salad with women." Erik shook

his head. "Not like us guys, huh, Max?"

"Oh, I actually ordered a salad too." Max laughed. "I guess she's rubbing off on me."

"I'm getting oysters." Erik wiggled his eyebrows. "I think I might find the woman of my dreams tonight with Samantha here as my good luck charm."

"Are you single?" I held back my thoughts about not being shocked that he might be.

"Yes, chronically, I'm afraid. Women just don't seem to enjoy my unique sense of humor." He shrugged. "Who knows why?"

"Jokes about hidden cameras might throw up some red flags." Max elbowed him.

"That it may, that it may." Erik grinned.

We placed our orders, then I cleared my throat. It was time to talk to Erik about the next book signing. I certainly didn't want it to go like the last one had. I just wasn't sure how open he'd be to altering his method of going with the flow.

"Erik, can I talk to you about something?" I met his eyes.

"Sure."

"Well, I was thinking about the next book signing, and I think it would be nice if we could plan that out a little bit."

"Oh, I have planned it out." He rubbed his hands together. "You're going to love it."

"Maybe you could give me a hint as to what to

expect?"

"That will ruin the surprise."

"Okay, but I'd really enjoy it if you would maybe give me a little input into the day. You see, I really want to make a good impression with my fans."

"You just have to trust me, Samantha. It's all going to be perfect."

"It's not that I don't trust you, it's just that there is so much that goes into a successful book signing. Since you're doing it all alone, I thought it might be good to be able to go over a few of the details with you before the actual event."

"I see." He chuckled. "So, you're not going to trust me at all?"

"I didn't say that. I just..." I sighed and closed my eyes for a moment. When I opened them again my food was right in front of me. Erik was already slurping one of his oysters. "I'm going to be honest with you, Erik. I believe in being as honest as possible at any given time. The truth is, I was really uncomfortable with how the last book signing went, and I'd like to be able to prevent that from happening again."

"Oh, doll." He leaned forward across the table and lowered his voice. "It's just because of all those vegetables you eat, you know. If you ease up on those, you probably won't be so gassy."

My mouth dropped open.

Max held his hand over his mouth, but I could still

hear him laugh.

I threw my napkin at him. "Shut up, Max!"

Max only laughed harder.

"Erik, that is not what I'm talking about!"

"No?" He slurped another oyster. "Fine, fine. If you must have it your way, then I'll tell you a little about what I have planned. It's going to be an outside venue. It's supposed to be beautiful that day, so I think it will be a perfect way to really change things up."

I waited for all of the reasons why I didn't like his idea to surface, but none came to mind.

"Actually, I think that's a really good idea. I could read a section of *Becoming Zara* that would be fitting for the outdoors. Then we'll be able to have the kind of impact on my fans that I'm hoping for—inspiration."

"Like I said, you're the boss."

"When did you say that exactly?" I raised an eyebrow.

"You just relax. I'm going to take care of everything. It will be perfect!"

CHAPTER 12

I did start to relax. I honestly believed that Erik would take care of things as he promised. So he'd made a few mistakes out of the gate; who didn't have an off day? Here he was, treating me to dinner, taking me out on the town to enjoy Amsterdam—he was clearly making an effort. Maybe if I did relax a bit more, it would turn out to be a fun night.

When I leaned over to take a bite of my salad, I experienced a strange sensation. It was as if I was being watched. I looked up to find Erik staring at me.

I wondered if it was a strange fetish of his to watch a woman eat. Why else would he stare so intently in my direction? I glanced over at Max to see if he'd noticed and found that he was staring at me just as intently. I raised an eyebrow.

"Did I drop something on my dress?" I looked down at my dress to see that half of my chest was exposed. The dress that had seemed undamaged when I'd put it on after my little mishap had apparently torn along the seam of the collar. I grabbed the flap of material and covered myself back up.

"Great." I sighed. "I guess I'll have to go change again."

"Not on my account." Erik winked.

"Seriously?" Max looked over at him.

"Okay, another bad joke." Erik laughed. "Don't worry, I can fix it." He reached into his pocket and pulled out a safety pin.

I didn't want to know why he had a safety pin in his pocket.

He walked over to me and expertly wound the pin through the tear in my dress. It worked just fine to cover up what the tear had exposed.

"Thanks, Erik."

He patted my shoulder. "You look beautiful."

When he sat back down again, he punctuated his statement by slurping an oyster into his mouth.

Max looked across the table at me. "Sammy, exactly what happened while you were getting dressed?"

"I'd really rather not talk about it."

"Hm." He quirked a brow and finished his food.

"Dessert," said Erik. "We absolutely have to have some dessert. I personally love chocolate ice cream."

"I'm okay, actually. I like to keep things light if I'm going dancing."

"I bet." Erik grinned. "You're probably wild on the dance floor, hm? I know your type. All uptight and proper most of the time, but then when you cut loose, you're just wild."

"Uh—I don't think I'm that uptight."

"Actually you're wrong there. Samantha is the furthest thing from wild." Max wiped his mouth. "I think I'll pass on ice cream too."

I tried not to show it, but I was a little hurt by Max's words. Did Max think I was as uptight as Erik did? It was true that I didn't cut loose very often, but that was because neither of us really did. Max certainly wasn't a party animal himself.

As I waited for the check to be delivered, I tried not to obsess over what Max had said. Surely, there were plenty of reasons that he'd made the comment. Most likely it was his attempt at defending me in front of Erik. *Don't read too much into it, Sammy.*

I cleared my throat and looked across the table at Max again. He smiled at me. But was it a real smile? Was it just what he did to keep me happy? How could he look forward to going out with someone who was never able to cut loose?

As we left the restaurant Max slid his arm around my waist. "He was right, you know."

"Who?"

"Erik."

"About what?"

He leaned close and whispered beside my ear. "You do look beautiful."

"Thanks." I smiled at him. "I hope you're up for this,

because I'm ready to have some real fun. I can't wait to get on that dance floor with you."

"Oh really?" He raised his eyebrows. "I wasn't expecting that. I figured we'd dance a few times and then call it a night."

"No way. We're in Amsterdam. I want to see what all the buzz is about."

"Oh?" Max grinned.

"Poor choice of words." I shook my head.

"We can stay as long as you want. I just thought you might need to rest."

I pursed my lips. There he went again, assuming that I was some old fuddy-duddy who couldn't hang with the cool crowd.

"The only thing I want is you and me having the time of our lives."

"Well, that should be pretty simple to arrange." He stole a kiss while Erik hailed a cab.

"Let's go, lovebirds!"

"This should be interesting." Max rolled his eyes.

"It will be." I had every intention of making sure that it was.

CHAPTER 13

The pounding music assaulted my ears the moment we opened the door. I cringed at the intensity of it. Maybe in my younger days blaring music gave me a thrill, but now I just wanted to ask someone to turn it down. Max, however, was looking eager to get on the dance floor. He pulled me straight toward it.

As the lights flashed and the music shifted from incessant thumping to something more melodic, I began to relax. Max's arms around me reminded me that anywhere could be perfect as long as we were together. The more we danced, the more relaxed I became. Time slipped by as if it didn't exist. The throb and pulse of the music settled my mind.

When I finally tore my eyes away from Max's for a moment, I noticed how crowded the dance floor was. I hadn't noticed all of the people gathering around us, but I was suddenly very uneasy. I moved closer to Max.

"I think I need a break. Can we sit down?"

"Sure." He started to guide me away from the crowd.

The people that surrounded us didn't seem inclined to move out of the way. In fact, there were a few who seemed to be intentionally standing in our way.

"Excuse me." I led with my elbow in an attempt to part the crowd.

"It *is* you! I thought it was you! My friend and I have been arguing about it for the past half hour. You owe me money, Nicole!"

"Alright, fine, you were right." The woman laughed.

Nicole was a gorgeous brunette who stood at least a foot taller than me.

I smiled at her. "I'd be happy to cover your debt."

"Oh, no need for that." She waved her hand. "It's just a hamburger. He bet me that it was you, I bet that it wasn't you, and whoever lost had to buy the other a hamburger."

"So it's a tasty bet."

"She's a bit obsessed with food." The man beside her leaned closer to me. "Anything she can do to get a free meal, you know?"

"Stop it, Cal, you're being so silly." Nicole rolled her eyes. "The truth is, I am really enjoying the food here. I know you're from the States. How do you like the food?"

"It's pretty great." I grimaced. "Though I am trying to watch the calories."

"Really?" Nicole tilted her head to the side. "Why?"

"I had a bit of a struggle with my weight."

"You look gorgeous."

"Thank you. So do you. But I didn't always, and I'd rather keep the weight off."

"Hm." Nicole shook her head. "You're going to have to loosen up a bit if you really want to enjoy Holland. The food is too good to pass up."

"Besides, there are plenty of ways to get a little exercise in around here." Cal shrugged. "We went on a bicycle tour today. It was fantastic."

"See, Max?" I nudged him with my elbow.

Max nodded, but he didn't smile or say a word.

"Here, this is the name of the tour we took." Nicole handed me a business card. "I highly recommend it. The tour guide made just riding the bicycle an adventure. He took us through some paths that were a little bumpy and curvy to get our blood pumping."

"Great. Thanks so much for this."

"Sammy, why don't we have one more dance?" Max started to steer me away from the couple.

"It was nice to meet you!" I smiled at them both.

Max pulled me into his arms and we began to dance again. I thought about asking him why he'd been so abrupt, but the moment we began moving together, the concern left my mind. Just as Nicole had reminded me, I needed to loosen up. I wanted to show Max that I could be as wild as he wanted.

When he started to spin me away from him, I lurched backward into a deep dip. Max held me steady, but as he pulled me back up, the safety pin that was holding my dress together popped off. The flap of dress that was torn fell away, revealing most of my bra.

"Oh no, Max!"

He pulled me hard against his chest to shield me. "Relax, no one saw." He kissed my cheek. "Just keep dancing."

"I don't know if I can like this."

"It's okay, I promise."

CHAPTER 14

I gritted my teeth and continued to dance. It was rather nice to be pinned against Max, but I spent the entire time nervous that someone would get a glimpse, or even worse, snap a picture of my wardrobe malfunction. I was so preoccupied with the thought that I forgot to pay attention to the movement of my feet.

I put one foot down hard on Max's. He grunted and tried to pull his foot back, but the motion set me off balance. I reached for his shoulder to steady myself, but when I did, the tear in my dress was revealed. I grabbed the material instead of his shoulder and stumbled backward several steps.

When I stepped on someone else's foot, I lurched to the side. My foot flew up from under me and I began to fall. I forgot about the flap of material as I swung my arms through the air in an attempt to catch myself.

It was too late. I hit the floor hard and bit my tongue in the same moment.

Throngs of people surrounded me. Some laughed.

Some appeared to want to help. Others just stared. No matter why they were looking at me, the point was that they were looking at me. I covered up as quickly as I could and stumbled to my feet.

Max squeezed his arm around my shoulders and looked into my eyes. "Are you alright?"

"Yes, I think so. I'm sorry. I didn't mean to cause such a commotion."

Max waved the onlookers away.

"Don't apologize. I'm sure that made you nervous. Do you want to call it a night?"

The question triggered anxiety within me. There it was. I'd been a killjoy again. There wasn't much chance that I would ever be able to change Max's opinion of me if I couldn't even handle a crowd.

"No, I'm okay. Let's keep dancing."

"Are you sure?" He brushed a strand of hair away from my face. "You were pretty freaked out."

"I don't want to call it a night, Max. I want to have fun."

"Okay." He smiled. "Then let's dance." He pulled me up against him in a swift sharp motion.

As he whipped and whirled me around with his body tight to mine, I laughed. The music mostly drowned it out, but it still shook my entire body. This was fun. This was letting go.

After several more dances, the music stopped.

"I guess they're closing…"

"Uh—I don't think so. Look." Max pointed toward the stage where the DJ was set up.

Instead of the DJ, Erik stood behind the mixing board. He waved to me and Max. Then he began to toy with the mixing board. As squeals and screeches filled the club, I worried that Erik may have had too much to drink. Why else would he think it was okay for him to be up on stage messing with the equipment?

"Where's the DJ?" I looked around for any sign of him.

"I'm sure he'll be back soon."

"Do you think we should go up there and get Erik?" I frowned.

"No, he's alright. He's just playing around. No one else seems to be surprised. Maybe he's done this before?"

"Hello, everyone. I'm DJ Erik and I'm here to tell you about an epic opportunity that we have coming up!"

I braced myself as he went into detail about the book signing. Just when I thought it couldn't get worse, he pointed me out in the middle of the dance floor.

"Come join us and you'll get some one-on-one attention from Samantha!"

My heart dropped. All eyes turned to me yet again. I was sure at least half of the people there had never heard of me before, but they had all seen me sprawled across the dance floor with my dress half off. Now Erik was promising them a chance for even more attention.

Still, I summoned a smile to my lips and greeted

everyone who looked in my direction. When the music started again I looked at Max. "This guy is going to kill me—you know that, right?"

"I can see he's pushing your buttons." He smiled. "But it's good publicity, right?"

I shook my head. "That's what this whole night was probably about—the chance to get me here so he could pull this publicity stunt. I just don't understand why he didn't tell me. I wouldn't have said no."

"Are you sure about that?" Max guided me off the dance floor. "It seems to me that you might have. You're not too thrilled with his ideas."

"Maybe you're right, but I should have the opportunity to decide that for myself." I frowned as we paused near the door. "Is it really so unreasonable that I prefer to know what to expect? I know that makes me boring, but I just can't get into the swing of letting things evolve as they will when it comes to my career."

"I think Erik is a challenge for you. I won't say his methods aren't unconventional. I can't even say that he doesn't irritate me. But I will say that you still have to work with him." He held the door open for me. "Let's not get into it tonight. Tomorrow we have the day off, and I'm sure that things will calm down after that."

"You're right. I'm looking forward to some down time with you—unless somehow Erik has plans to turn that into a publicity stunt too."

CHAPTER 15

After a refreshing night's sleep, I woke up eager to discover what the day ahead held in store for us. Max was less chipper, but came around after a breakfast of fresh fruit, fresh coffee, and perfectly cooked eggs.

As we left the restaurant, I pulled out the card for the bicycle tour.

"It's not too far away. We can walk to it." I looped my arm through his. "I'm so glad that I'm going to get to experience this with you."

Max nodded. He cleared his throat. "You know, I'm feeling a little off."

"You are?" I looked over at him. "Mentally or physically?"

"I'm not sure yet."

We arrived at the bicycle tour office just in time to join in the next tour.

"I'll find us some bikes. Why don't you sit down and rest for a few minutes?"

"Okay." He nodded and sat down on a bench not far

from the door.

I walked through the office and was guided out the back by the tour operator.

"You can choose from those bicycles." He pointed to a group near the door. "Once you pick one, we can adjust it to suit you."

I looked through the bicycles. It didn't take me long to find a flashy emerald one. Max's was more subdued in a cobalt shade of blue.

While mine was being adjusted, I wheeled Max's around to the front of the office so that he could take a look. He was still sitting on the bench, hunched over.

"Max, I got you a bike. Do you like it?"

He looked at the bicycle and nodded. "It's fine. It's a little big, don't you think?"

"It's the same size as mine. The guide will adjust it to fit you. Do you want something smaller?"

He grimaced and shoved his hands into his pockets. "Sammy, I'm not sure if I feel up to biking."

"What's wrong?" I looked into his eyes. "Are you sick?"

"Maybe a little. My stomach feels off. Maybe I drank too much last night. I'd just rather not bike right now."

"That's fine. We can sign up for a tour later in the day. They do one every three hours. Do you want to go back to the room?"

"I do. But you should bike. I know you've been looking forward to it. Just keep your cell phone on and don't talk to strangers."

"I see you haven't lost your sense of humor." I smiled at him. "I'd rather spend my time with you."

"But you have the signing tomorrow. I don't want you to miss out on a day of fun because of me." He stood up and wrapped his arm around my waist. "Go ride like the wind. I'll be waiting for you when you get back."

"Are you sure? I really don't like the idea of leaving you behind."

"Trust me, I don't mind." He smiled.

I searched his eyes. Something was off. I knew it was. "Max, what's going on?"

"Nothing. Like I said, I just need a little rest. Please, I'll feel awful if I think that you missed out on something because of me." He paused a moment and then met my eyes. "Just be careful."

"I will be." I kissed his cheek. "Get some good rest, okay?"

"I will."

I climbed onto the bicycle and joined a crowd of other bicyclists who were participating in the tour. It made me uneasy to think of Max all alone, but if it was what he wanted, then I didn't have much of a choice.

As the tour began, I tried to focus on the words of the guide. The beauty that I passed by was enthralling to me, but after a few minutes my mind drifted back to Max.

What was he doing? Was he sleeping? He didn't have much hair to hold back, but I could at least put a cool rag on his forehead or feed him crackers. A pang of guilt slowed me down. He shouldn't be alone.

I started to turn back, but before I could, a rush of cyclists pedaled past me. I waited for the long parade to subside. Navigating the bicycle traffic seemed harder than navigating car traffic.

When I finally began to pedal again, I noticed a small group riding on their own. The tour was nice, but I could see how going off by myself would be nice too. I decided to take a tour of my own on my way back.

I turned down side streets and explored as far as I could. It didn't take long for me to realize that I was lost. I tried to use the GPS on my cell phone, but it was directing me in circles. My heart pounded as I wondered how I'd get back. I knew I could call Max, but since he was sick, I didn't want to bother him. There was only one other option.

I sighed and dialed Erik's number. I expected to leave a message, but to my surprise he picked up on the second ring.

"How is your day of exploring going?"

"I think I may have explored a little too far."

"Oh? Is something wrong?"

"I might be just a little bit lost."

"Do you have any idea of where you are?"

"Near a coffee shop, I think."

"That is really not helpful." He laughed.

I had to laugh with him. "Good point. My GPS says

I'm in the middle of the Bermuda Triangle."

"Hm. What about Max's phone? Does it have any better directions?"

"Max isn't here. He was feeling a little sick."

"You're alone?"

"Yes."

"I'll be right there."

"How?" I laughed. "You don't even know where I am."

"Oh, right. Go into the coffee shop and ask the owner for the address. That should give us a starting point."

"Thanks, Erik."

"No problem. Call me right back when you have it."

"Okay." I hung up the phone and stepped into the coffee shop. It was quite crowded and had a very noticeable scent.

CHAPTER 16

When I walked up to the counter at the coffee shop, the owner met my eyes.

"Would you like to see the menu?"

"No, thank you. I'm a little turned around and I'm hoping you can give me the name of the street I'm on."

"I can do better than that." He snapped his fingers and a man walked over to the bar. "Can you please escort this woman home?"

"Oh no, that won't be necessary, I have a bicycle and—"

"And it will fit just fine in the trunk." The man, who appeared to be in his fifties, nodded to me. "I'll get you back to your hotel safe."

"I'm not staying in a hotel, actually. I'm staying in a container."

"What?" The man behind the counter laughed.

"Who talked you into that?" The older man grinned.

I rolled my eyes. "It's a long story."

"Alright, I'll take you back to your container."

"Thank you." I smiled at how absurd it sounded.

"Here—for the road." The man behind the counter handed me a small package.

"Oh no, thank you. I don't want anything from the menu."

"Oh, this isn't from the menu, it's from my personal stash." He winked at me. "Just cookies."

"Oh yum, thank you!"

He nodded.

Once my bicycle was stowed in the trunk, the driver took me right back to the container, with one stop at the guided tour to return the bicycle.

I felt a little silly, as I was apparently only about five minutes away from the office. Some explorer I'd turned out to be.

"How much do I owe you?" I reached into my purse for my wallet.

"No charge."

"Really? Why?"

He smiled at me. "I know there's only one man in Amsterdam that would have set you up in a shipping container. Erik, right?"

My eyes widened. "How did you know?"

"Erik is pretty well known around here. He likes to call himself inventive, but really he just has a reputation for being outlandish. Every event he plans ends up turning into quite a fiasco."

"I think I'd have to agree with that."

"He might be difficult, but in the long run I've never

seen one of his events fail. However, this container thing…" He laughed. "That's a new level of inventive for him."

"It's been interesting, that's for sure."

I stepped out of the car and walked up to the door. When I opened it, I found Max perched on the tiny couch with his arm high in the air and a tablet aimed at his face.

"Max, what are you doing?"

He jumped when he heard my voice and the tablet slipped out of his hand and struck him right in the face. "Ouch!"

"Oh no, I'm so sorry. I didn't mean to startle you. Are you okay? Do you want me to get you some ice?"

He pinched the top of his nose as he sat up on the couch. "No, it's fine."

"It's really not." I sat down beside him and tried to peer at the damage. "You're already sick and now you're injured."

"Ah, Sammy, I have to be honest with you."

"What is it?" I frowned.

"I'm not really sick. Though I do feel awful for lying to you."

"What? Why would you lie to me about that?"

He sighed and rubbed his nose. "It was stupid, I know."

"Let me get you some ice."

"I'm fine, really. It's hard to get a signal in here."

"I know. I'm not sure if this place is going to work out."

"Sammy, I hate that I missed time with you today. I guess that you cut your tour short?"

"I wanted to be with you, even if it wasn't on the tour. But I guess maybe you needed some time alone. I forget that sometimes too much togetherness is too much."

"Why would you think that?" Max narrowed his eyes.

"Well, you did fake being sick to get away from me." I looked away from him.

He reached out and took my hand in his. "Don't think that. That's not what I did. I never want to get away from you, Sammy."

"Then why?"

He grimaced and looked down at the tablet that had landed on the couch. "It's nothing, really."

"Max, what are you keeping from me?" I stroked his cheek. "I can tell when you're hiding something. You get a little twitch in your eyebrow, and you tighten your lips as if you're afraid you're going to let the secret spill."

He looked up at me. "You know me too well."

"I love you because I know you so well. Just spill, so your eyebrow can stop twitching."

He reached up and rubbed his eyebrow. "It's nothing to be concerned about."

"Any time there's dishonesty between us, that's always a concern."

"Well, I wouldn't go that far. I don't always have to share every personal detail of my life. Do I?" He looked into my eyes. "It's okay to have a few secrets."

I held my breath in reaction to his words. What kind of secret might he have? What happened that he wasn't willing to share with me? Was it my controlling nature rearing its head again, or were my instincts right?

"Max, I agree that you're entitled to some secrets, but I just hope that you know I'm here for you. No matter how busy I am, no matter what I'm wrapped up in, I'm always one hundred percent available to you. Okay?" I looked into his eyes.

"Sammy, I know that. I don't want to make you think I don't. Honestly, it's just a little embarrassing."

"Well, you've seen my every embarrassing moment, so I don't know why that would be a problem."

"Can I just have this?" He shook his head. "I just don't want to share it. Okay? There's some things that I just don't want to share. I don't know why that has to be a problem."

I sighed and looked away from him. It was clear that he wanted to remain strong about this. If I pushed, he'd probably give in and tell me, but that would just prove what Erik claimed—that I was wound far too tight.

"It's not a problem. You're right. Obviously you didn't want to do the bike tour, but you said that you don't need time away from me. So maybe we can do something different? Say, hunt down that museum we missed out on yesterday?"

"The Stedelijk? I think that's a great idea."

"Alright, now will you let me see your nose?" He pulled his hand away to reveal a red mark. "No bruise yet."

"I think I'll be okay." He smiled.

CHAPTER 17

Hand in hand, Max and I walked toward the museum. Even though I'd told him it was fine, my mind was spinning with curiosity. What would Max possibly need to keep from me? Was it something that I'd done? Was it something that he thought I was too uptight to understand?

I grimaced at the thought. The number one priority in my relationship with Max was honesty. I always wanted him to be able to tell me anything. Now it seemed that I'd failed at that goal. There was clearly something that he didn't want to tell me.

When we reached the museum Max looked over at me. "You haven't said a word. Are you sure we're okay?"

"Always." I kissed his cheek. "Let's lose ourselves in some beautiful art."

"Yes, let's." He smiled and opened the door for me.

The first painting we studied was a beautiful couple dancing across an opulent dance floor. Every detail was splashed with gold.

"They look like they're having a good time." I gazed at the painting.

"No different than us last night."

"It looks like they're in a palace."

"I'm always in a palace when I'm with you."

I turned to look at him with a raised eyebrow. "Really?"

"Really." He offered a wide smile.

"Hm." I turned back to the painting. "I'm not sure that I could ever call the container a palace."

We moved on to the next painting. Right away I noticed that it was designed around a single focal point—a rusted abandoned bicycle on the side of the road.

"Quite poetic."

"A piece of garbage?" He shook his head. "I'm sorry, I don't get it."

"Well I think maybe the artist intended to represent human life with the bicycle."

"So why not just use a human being? I mean how is human life anything like a bicycle."

"Well, we keep going until we can't any more."

"But we don't run with chains and gears. I get what you're saying, I just think a bicycle was a poor choice."

"What would you choose?" I studied him intently. I tried to take every chance I had to get to know Max better.

"I don't know—maybe a car, a vehicle of some kind. Or maybe just a rusty old human."

"That might be a bit harsh to see."

"But it would be the truth, right? I guess that's why I've never really understood art. I prefer to be able to look at something and just understand it, instead of all these strange images that I'm supposed to be able to interpret. That's a lot of work. If you want to represent the ebbing of human life, then just do that."

"I'm not sure that people would want a painting like that hanging over their mantle."

"But that's my point." He frowned. "Either way it's the same message. So what's the point of trying to make it look pretty?"

"Or maybe it's just the bicycle." I met his eyes. "Is that the problem?"

"What? Why would it be?"

I wagged a finger at him. "I'm getting to the bottom of things. First, you didn't want to go on the bicycle tour, now you're getting all annoyed by a painting of a bicycle. What is going on, Max?"

"I thought you said you were going to let this go?" He sighed and stepped away from the painting.

"I did. But it doesn't seem to me that you're letting it go. What's bothering you?"

"I knew that you wouldn't be able to drop this."

"I'm sorry. I just can't. I know that something has you upset and I just want to know what it is. We always work through everything together. Is it such a bad thing that I want to work through this together too?"

"What if there isn't a way to work through it? What if the only thing I can do is learn to live with it?"

The question horrified me. What was it that Max thought he had to learn to live with? It seemed to me that the only thing that had changed was our marriage.

"Max, is it something about me? Because I can change."

He sighed heavily and shook his head. "No, it's nothing about you, Samantha. Not at all. I wish you wouldn't always think that."

"Then what is it?"

He grabbed me by the elbow and steered me off to the side. We sat down on a small bench.

CHAPTER 18

Max took a deep breath. "Okay, the truth is that you're right as usual. It is about the bikes."

"What is it? Do you have some kind of rash?" I scrunched up my nose.

"No, I don't have a rash." He rolled his eyes. "I don't want to admit this, but I'm afraid to ride a bike."

I stared at him for a long moment. "What are you talking about? We've gone biking together before."

"I know. But there was an incident."

"An incident?" I raised an eyebrow.

"Yes. It happened back when you were occupied with the book. Remember, I went on that bike race?"

"Yes. You said you had a good time."

"Well, that wasn't the entire truth." He looked down at his feet and then back up at me. "You were just so stressed with the book stuff, and nothing really happened, so I didn't want to worry you."

"Max, what is it? What happened?"

"I had a close call with a car. I wasn't hit, or hurt, but

when I saw it coming straight at me, I was terrified." He sighed and rubbed a hand along his chin. "At first, I thought I was just taking a break—that I'd be able to get back to riding when I had the chance. But the next time I tried to get on the bike, I couldn't do it. I just kept seeing that car."

"Oh Max, this is so great!" I clapped my hands.

"Huh?" His eyes widened. "What's so great about it, Sammy?"

"I'm sorry, I didn't mean it like that. You're right, there isn't anything great about you being scared. But what is great about it is that I will get to help you with something. You're always the one standing by me and helping me through a crisis. Now I get to help you." I smiled. "That's something I am excited about."

"No, there's no need. It's not a crisis. It's just a personal preference. I don't want to ride bikes any more, so I won't." He shrugged and shoved his hands in his pockets. "There's not really anything more to say about it, I don't think."

"Oh, Max, don't be like that. Think of all of the times I wanted to do things and was too scared. You helped me through that fear." I tugged one of his hands out of his pocket and held it in my own.

"There's a difference here, Sammy. I don't want to do it. I don't need to. I'm perfectly fine moving on with my life, with this one little thing that I can't do."

"Max, we're here in Amsterdam. Everyone rides a

bike. It's the safest place you're ever going to get back on a bike. Why not just try?" I leaned forward and kissed his cheek. "Giving up on something you enjoyed just because you're a little afraid is not a good thing to do."

"It's not a big deal, Sammy. Why are you trying to turn it into one?"

"Because it is a big deal, Max. Giving in to fear is a huge deal."

"Stop." He sighed. "You're blowing this out of proportion. I'm just not going to ride a bike—what?"

"It's not about the bike, Max." I bit into my bottom lip. From the edgy way he was looking at me and the tension in his jaw it was easy for me to assume that he was upset. I didn't want to make him feel any worse.

"If I'd given into my fear, we would not even be together, Max. Giving in to fear is a very dangerous thing. After everything that you've done for me, please let me do this one thing for you. I know if you let me, I can help you through this."

He grimaced. "It really means a lot to you, hm?"

"More than you could ever know." I clasped my hands together and looked into his eyes.

"I'll try, Sammy. That's all I can promise. I'm not sure that I can do it, but for you, I will try."

"That's all I'm asking." I gave him a quick peck on the cheek. "We'll go tomorrow, in the morning before the book signing. There will be less traffic and plenty of space for us to overcome that fear of yours."

"I believe you." He laughed a little. "It's funny. I never thought I'd believe it. But when you say that you'll get me through this, I truly do believe you."

As we continued through the rest of the museum, my mind churned with excitement. Not only did Max open up to me, but now I knew a way that I could help him. I was sure it wouldn't take much to get him back on the bike again.

CHAPTER 19

Early the next morning I tried to get out of bed without waking Max. I wanted a few minutes to meditate before we went out on our bike riding expedition. As I tried to crawl over him, not waking him seemed to be impossible. There just wasn't enough room. My foot slid on the sheets and I ended up straddled across him.

"Wow, what a way to wake up." He grinned.

"Ha, ha. I'm stuck." I pouted.

"Just roll off, I'll catch you."

"No, I'm really stuck. Look." I pointed to my foot, crammed between the bed and the wall.

"Ah, so you're my captive?" He reached out and tickled my stomach.

"Max!" I squealed and managed to get my foot free. When I rolled off Max, he was too busy trying to tickle me to remember to catch me. I ended up in a pile on the floor. "Ouch."

"Sorry!" Max jumped up and helped me to my feet. "I didn't think you'd launch off like that without a warning."

"It's okay. I'm okay, really. This just makes us even for the tablet incident."

"Good point." He rubbed the bridge of his nose. "Are you sure we have to get up? Maybe we should just sleep in for a bit. We might never get to sleep in a bed this small again. It gives me plenty of excuse to snuggle." He held out his hand to me.

I grabbed it and smirked. "Oh no, you're not getting out of this one. We're going to overcome that fear today. Plus, you never need an excuse to snuggle."

I tugged on his hand hard until he sat up.

"Alright, alright, I'll give it a try." He grabbed some clothes. "I'll go change in the bathroom so you'll have room to change. Just try not to hurt yourself."

I would have laughed if it weren't a valid warning. Once Max left, I pulled on some athletic pants and a loose t-shirt. I was prepared to do whatever it took to get him back on a bicycle.

I stepped out the door and found Max just outside. "Ready?"

"Not really." He crossed his arms. "Are you sure that I can't talk you out of this?"

"I'm sure. Just give it a chance, Max. If it's not me, who will it be?"

"No one. That's kind of the point."

"Ha, ha." I grinned.

We didn't have to walk far to find a shop that rented bicycles. As we looked through the options, I noticed

Max could barely keep his hands still. When he saw me looking in his direction, he shoved his hands deep into his pockets.

"What do you think, Max?"

"I don't know—you pick one."

"I really think you should pick your own. Maybe a smaller bicycle that you can feel you have more control over. Or something in a neutral color?"

"Sammy, it doesn't matter which bicycle it is. I'm not going to feel safe getting on it. What are you going to do? Hold on to the back and run me down the street?" He laughed. "I'm sorry. I just don't think this is going to work."

I wanted to argue his point, but it was a good one. I couldn't exactly assure him that he would be safe when he would be out of my control. Just when I thought I should give up and let Max give in to his fear, I noticed the perfect bicycle.

"That's it!" I pointed to a tandem bicycle leaning against the wall. "It's perfect!"

"Are you kidding? It's huge."

"That's because it's a bicycle built for two. Max, I'll be with you the entire time. That should help with your fear."

The owner walked over to us. "How can I help you?"

"We'd like to rent this bike." I pointed it out to him.

"Oh, that bike?" He shook his head. "No, I don't think that's the right bike for you. Two separate bikes would be better."

"Really, we have to have this one. You see, my husband—"

Max cleared his throat. I realized that he probably didn't want me telling this stranger about his bicycle phobia. "—We just want to have a good day together. This would be so romantic." I smiled. "Please?"

The owner looked between the two of us. "You're not going to go too far?"

"No, just an easy ride—probably through the park."

He frowned. "I really shouldn't."

"Oh, please do. I really would like to try this out."

Finally he nodded. "Alright, you can take the bike. Let me just get the paperwork."

As he walked away, I turned to face Max and clapped my hands. "Yes! In no time at all you're going to be having a great time on a bike again."

"Sammy, I appreciate what you're trying to do here, but I hope you won't be too disappointed if things don't turn out the way that you want them to."

"I'm going to be fine, Max. As long as you're willing to try, that's all that matters. Even if we're only on the bike for two minutes, that's a start."

"It might be one minute." Max cringed.

I signed the papers that the owner offered me, then smiled at Max. "Don't worry, you're going to love this."

I wheeled the tandem bicycle out of the shop and out onto the street. "We'll start off in the park so there's nothing to spook you."

When we entered the park there were many other bikers on the paths. Some were riding just as fast as cars. I looked around for a more isolated area.

"Here we go, this is a good place. I'll get on first so that I can hold the bicycle steady. Then you can get on next."

"Sammy, I think this is a bad idea." Max wiped his hands along his jeans.

I mounted the front seat of the bicycle and looked over at him. "It's only scary until you're on the bike again. Then it won't seem so bad."

He looked at me with doubt in his eyes, but he climbed onto the back seat of the bicycle.

With very easy movements we practiced pedaling just a few feet before stopping.

"It's pretty wobbly." Max frowned.

"It will get easier as we go faster."

"Faster? I don't like the sound of that."

"Have faith, Max—faith!"

After a few rounds in the park, I slowed the bicycle to a stop. "How are you feeling, Max?"

"Pretty good." He smiled. "It wasn't as bad as I thought. I mean, I can't complain about the view."

"Yes, this park is pretty, isn't it?"

"That's not the view I'm talking about." He laughed.

I looked over my shoulder and realized what he referring to. "Oh, very sweet, Max. Now let's take this ride out onto the road."

"The road? Are you sure?"

"We'll be fine."

CHAPTER 20

I steered the bicycle out of the park and onto one of the main roads. In Amsterdam, bicycles had the right of way, and since there were so many, riding on the road seemed safe. Once we got the right pattern going with our pedaling we began to fly down the road.

Max was quiet behind me. I didn't like that I couldn't see his face, but I thought he would be more comfortable in the back. As we rode further along the road there were many sights to see. I slowed down to look at some of the architecture of the old stacked buildings.

"How are you doing back there, Max?" I took a look over my shoulder.

"Sammy! Eyes on the road!"

The brief glimpse I'd gotten of Max revealed to me that his skin was quite pale and his hands were curled around the handlebars very tightly.

"Don't worry, I'm going to take good care of you, Max. Nothing bad is going to happen."

I continued to pedal, only a little bit faster. I wanted

him to feel the wind as it blew through his hair. I wanted him to experience that sensation of weightlessness that came with a good coast on a bicycle.

The faster I pedaled, the narrower the road seemed to become. I tried to slow down a little but we were on a hill. As my heart began to pound faster, I realized that I might have been going too fast and underestimated just how much weight was on our two-person bicycle. Even though I slowed my pedaling, the bicycle still raced down the hill. It gained speed with every second that passed.

"Sammy! Too fast! You have to slow down, please!"

I could hear the strain in Max's voice. I didn't want him to think that anything was wrong, but something was very wrong. The brakes seemed to be doing nothing to slow us. At the bottom of the hill I thought things would calm down, but instead the bicycle continued to race forward.

There was some traffic up ahead—traffic that had no clue a tandem bicycle was about to collide with it. I had promised Max that nothing bad would happen. Now we were both going to end up in the hospital—if we were lucky enough to make it through.

As the bicycle hit a bump I gulped back a cry of fear. I clung to the handlebars and wondered just why I'd insisted on riding a bike.

The bicycle lurched to the left. I tried to correct it and only ended up tilting to the right.

"Sammy! What are you doing?"

I didn't have time to think about how upset Max was. All I could see was the traffic we were about to crash into. With nowhere left to go I turned the bicycle hard to the left. At least we would be out of the traffic pattern, even if we were bumped and scraped up. However, what I didn't account for was the canal right beside the road—the beautiful canal that I'd made a wish into just hours before. Now it betrayed me.

"Samantha!" Max shrieked and then gurgled.

I sealed my mouth shut and my eyes closed as we plunged into the canal with the bicycle wheels still spinning. The water wasn't as cold as I expected. That was a good thing. In a state of shock, I sank down through the water. It didn't occur to me to swim up. It didn't dawn on me that soon I would need to take another breath. Instead, I could only process that I was under the water, and Max was going to be furious.

I felt a hand wrap around my wrist and tug. Only then did I realize that I needed to swim. Max and I swam up together to the surface of the canal.

As I gulped for air people at the edge of the canal shouted.

"Are you okay? Someone help them!"

Max took deep breaths and clung to my wrist.

We swam to the edge of the canal.

"I'm sorry." I looked over at him.

He only shook his head. "I'll give you a boost. We need to get out of this water."

I tried to climb up out of the canal but it was slippery, I was slippery, and it seemed that everyone in Amsterdam was staring at us. Max shoved hard at my waist in an attempt to be polite, but when I slid down for the third time, he groaned. His palms dug into my rear end and he gave another fierce shove. I pulled up as hard as I could and flopped onto the side of the canal.

Max was still in the water.

I turned back and reached for him with both hands. He didn't take as much tugging.

Once he was out of the water he helped me to my feet.

"Are you hurt?" He met my eyes.

"No. I don't think so. Are you?"

"No." He wrung out the bottom of his shirt. "Can we give up on biking now?"

I frowned. "I'm so sorry, Max."

The crowd around us dispersed as people realized that help was no longer needed.

Max didn't even look at me. My stomach ached with how badly I felt. I'd insisted on him participating in something that he was frightened of, and in the end I'd probably traumatized him even further. How did I ask forgiveness for that?

"I really am sorry, Max."

"I know." He sighed. "It's not a big deal."

"It is. It really is." I took his hand in mine.

"Let's just go back to the rental place. We'll have to

tell them about the bicycle."

"I'll just pay for it."

"I know." He sighed. His jaw tensed.

I knew he had something to say.

"It's okay if you're upset with me, Max. You have a right to be."

He slicked his wet hair back over his head and lifted his eyes back to mine. "Alright, I am upset."

"I'm sorry."

"I know that—which is why I don't want to be upset. I know that you didn't do it on purpose."

"I really didn't." I lowered my eyes.

"But I told you that I didn't want to bike at all."

"I should have listened to you."

"Why did you go so fast?" He stared at me. "Were you trying to make me scream? Or did you want to tease me?"

"No, Max, that wasn't it at all."

"Then what happened?"

"The hill. The hill came up and I didn't expect it. Then we started going so fast and no matter what I did I couldn't slow us down. We were about to head into traffic. I didn't think about the canal being there. I'm so sorry, Max."

"Hey." He gave my hand a squeeze. "I can't say I'm happy about it, but like I said, I know you didn't do it on purpose. Let's just head back and get changed. Maybe find some less risky activities to engage in. Okay?"

"I guess." I wrung out my own shirt as we walked.

We were the only people on the street that were soaked from head to toe.

CHAPTER 21

Max and I were almost back to the rental when I heard a familiar voice.

"If you were going swimming you should have invited me! I would have joined in." Erik laughed as he walked up to us.

I cringed. "It's really not funny. I almost drowned Max."

"I didn't almost drown."

"Well, you know—every couple fights." Erik smiled and looked between us. "I'm sure that by tomorrow all will be forgotten."

"We weren't fighting. We were biking." I sighed. "I guess I went down a hill far too fast."

"What about the brakes?" Erik raised an eyebrow. "That should have stopped you."

"I tried them, but I guess I was going too fast."

"Wait a minute. Who did you rent from?" He crossed his arms.

"Bike Now. We rented a tandem bicycle."

"Oh, no. Not the tandem." He shook his head. "I thought it might be. I'm coming with you to the rental office."

"I don't think that's such a good idea." I shook my head. "It's my fault. We're just going to offer to pay for the bicycle and whatever service is needed to get the bicycle out of the canal."

"You'll do no such thing." For once Erik's voice sounded stern. It was so out of character for him that it surprised me.

"What do you mean?"

"You just let me handle this."

I opened my mouth to argue, but thought better of it. I was curious about why Erik's attitude had changed so much. Maybe this was a side of him that I wanted to see.

He walked with us back to the rental office. When we arrived, I spotted the owner outside. He was speaking to someone and from the tension in his face, I guessed that he might have heard about the accident.

"I feel awful. I hope this doesn't cause him too much trouble."

"Oh, it's going to cause him trouble alright." Erik narrowed his eyes and stormed up to the man. "What is the meaning of this, Gerard?"

"What?" Gerard looked at Erik, then past him at me and Max.

"Should we stop him?" I glanced over at Max.

"No, I don't think so. He seems to know what he's

doing."

"Maybe, but he seems so angry. That's not exactly a good way to apologize."

"Erik, I'm sorry. I didn't mean for this to happen." The owner hung his head.

"But it did—just like I warned you it would. These are my guests, Gerard, and now they've had an awful time because of you."

I raised an eyebrow and studied Gerard's expression. Instead of being angry that his bicycle was deep in a canal, he looked nervous.

"I didn't think they would go far with it. I figured they'd keep to the bicycle paths."

"That bicycle was not safe to be on the road and you know it. I warned you that the brakes were no good— that they needed to be repaired. I told you not to put the bicycle up for rent until you fixed it."

"I'm sorry. I know. But it's what she wanted, and I didn't want to disappoint her—and I didn't think it would be a problem." He grumbled his words and kept his eyes to the ground.

"The brakes were bad?" I stared at Gerard. "You let me take my husband out on a broken bicycle?"

"It wasn't broken. It just needed to be tweaked a bit. I'm so sorry. I wish it hadn't happened."

"That's not good enough. We could have been hurt or worse." Max scowled at him. "How could you do that?"

"Be prepared, Gerard, they can ensure that your shop is closed." Erik shook his head. "I'll make sure that it is."

"Please, don't do that. It's all I have. I didn't repair the bicycle because I didn't have the funds to do it. I was going to have it repaired as soon as I could."

I closed my eyes and recalled the way that Gerard had tried to talk me into a different bicycle. Of course he could have just told me that the bicycle was broken, and I would have gladly chosen a different one, but he had at least made an effort to redirect my attention.

"That's not necessary. It's really not." I frowned and looked at Max. "No one got hurt, right?"

"You can't be serious." Max looked into my eyes. "This man was beyond reckless."

"And I'm sure that this incident will be lesson enough for him to change his ways. Is that right, Gerard?" I looked back at him.

"Oh yes, of course. I will never rent that bicycle out again."

"Because it's at the bottom of a canal." Erik rolled his eyes. "Samantha, there's no need to be nice. He did something terrible and he should be punished for it."

"I agree that it was terrible, but I'm sure there is some other solution that we can come to. I think if we worked together we could reach an acceptable plan. A man shouldn't lose his business over one mistake. As long as Gerard agrees to have all of his bicycles inspected and to always do a safety check before renting out his bicycles, then I think we can let this go. Don't you think, Max?"

Max tightened his lips. He took a deep breath and looked into my eyes. "Is that what you think is best?"

"I do." I frowned. "I am still a bit at fault, after all. I did pedal much faster than I should have been with you on the bicycle."

He smiled at me. "Sometimes I am amazed by you, Sammy."

I winked at him and looked back at Gerard. "Is it a deal?"

"Oh yes, absolutely."

"And Erik, you can hold him to it?"

Erik stared at me with wide eyes. He nodded. "Yes. I can do that."

"Now, let's go get changed, Max. We still have some free time left."

As I turned to walk away, Erik caught up with me.

"Wait just a second, Samantha."

"Yes?" I met his eyes.

"I just have to say that you surprised me."

"I have to say, ending our bike ride in a canal surprised me too." I laughed a little.

Max did not.

"What I mean to say is, I didn't think you'd be so relaxed about this whole incident. I was sure that you'd have Gerard's business closed."

"Well, maybe you don't know as much as you think you do about me, Erik." I shrugged. "Sometimes I do stress over the small things, I'll admit it. Sometimes I get worked up to the point of boiling over when things are not going as planned. But when it comes to a man's business, that's not something I take lightly. I didn't intend to ride Max right into the canal, and I'm sure Gerard didn't intend for us to end up there either. People make mistakes. We have to accept that, or we'll all go mad."

"Interesting." He smiled at me a little more. "Thanks for the insight."

"I'll see you later for the book signing?"

"Absolutely."

CHAPTER 22

Max swung my hand back and forth as we walked toward the container. "You really are a good person, Sammy."

"Seriously?" I grinned at him. "Even after our unplanned bath?"

"You took the time to try to help me with my fear. That was thoughtful. You took the time to understand why Gerard may have made the mistake he did. That was thoughtful."

"Maybe, but I didn't exactly respect your wishes when it came to your not wanting to bike in the first place. If I had, then none of this would have happened."

"That's true, but it doesn't change the fact that you were right. I am going to have to get over my fear. Now, though, I might have to get over a fear of swimming too."

"Oh no, Max!" I groaned.

"And probably a fear of Amsterdam."

I rolled my eyes. "Stop!"

"Definitely a fear of people named Gerard!"

I gave him a playful shove.

He wrapped me up in his arms and swung me around to face him. "Never doubt for a second that you are the best influence in my life, Sammy."

Dazzled, as always, by the intensity of my gratitude for the opportunity to love and be loved by Max, I leaned in and kissed him. In the middle of Amsterdam, where anything could and did happen, all that mattered was his lips tangled with mine.

He tugged me inside and started to peel off my wet clothing. I did the same for him. For the first time since we'd been pinned together inside the shipping container, I didn't think about what my body might look like to him. I embraced him without question. Once we were free of our wet clothes we rummaged around for something dry to wear.

Max pulled me back to him. "We have some time, don't we?"

"No, not enough." I laughed.

I didn't think about whether that laughter made the rolls of my stomach shake, or whether it was too loud and unladylike. I didn't think about anything but the smile on my husband's face. In that instant, I realized that there *were* moments when I relaxed fully. Those moments were always with Max.

I pulled on fresh clothes, then waited—or more accurately, watched—while Max finished dressing.

"Ready?" He reached for my hand.

"I'm not so sure, to be honest."

"What's wrong? You weren't hurt in the canal, were you?"

"No, I wasn't. It's Erik. Every time I'm around him, my nerves are on edge. There's something about him that ruffles every one of my feathers."

"Oh, babe, you haven't figured that out yet?"

"What?"

He smiled. "He's too casual for you."

"Casual? You mean unpredictable and unorganized?"

"Sure, if you want to call it that. He plucks your nerves because he's the opposite of you. He's going to keep plucking them until we leave Amsterdam."

"That really doesn't make me feel any better." I sighed.

"Nothing I can say will make you feel better. But you could try a new tactic with him."

"What's that?"

"Just don't argue. It's his book signing. He is the host, right?"

"Yes." I frowned. "But it's my reputation."

"I think it's more his than yours in this case. He's the one responsible for organizing the event. I'm sure most people would pin the success or failure of the event on him, not you."

"But I don't feel comfortable with that."

Max took a step closer to me. "Why is that?" He looked into my eyes.

"I think that's more than clear. This is my career. I can't just let it go to pieces because of one guy's unique ideas."

"I don't recall it going to pieces. When did that happen?"

"Max, you know what I mean. It's just better if I know what's going to happen next."

"Or maybe, I'm not the only one with a fear that needs to be faced." He brushed his fingertip across his nose. "You're afraid to let go of control."

I clenched my jaw and stopped myself from spouting off an irrational reply. If anyone else said those words to me, I would have argued to the point of exhaustion. But Max's opinion meant more to me than anyone else's did. My urge to rush into a defensive state was calmed by the warmth in his eyes.

"I guess I am afraid of losing it all."

He stroked his fingers down along the curve of my cheek. "I know you are. You've gotten what you wanted, and now all you can see are ways that you might lose it all down the road."

"Yes." I frowned. "One mistake could ruin everything."

"As long as you believe that, maybe it could. But I know you better than that, Sammy. Deep down, you know that it would take a lot more than one mistake to derail you now."

I glanced at my watch. "We really have to go."

"Just something to think about." He kissed my cheek. "Let's go see what Erik has in store for us."

CHAPTER 23

It started out just fine. The park itself was quite large and open. I took a deep breath of the fresh air and was inspired by it. Yes, an outdoor reading could be just what I needed. It would give me a chance to reconnect with nature while also attempting to relinquish control.

With Max's hand in mine, I walked through the archway into a lush garden. The green grass against the endless backdrop of blue sky was enough to make me think I'd stepped right into a flawless painting. When I walked toward the center of the park, I noticed that there were more benches scattered around.

In what appeared to be the most central place, the ground was dotted with cushions that disturbed the natural feel of things. The cushions were covered in a flower pattern but still didn't quite reach the point of blending into the natural environment. I had to fight the urge to pick them up and stack them in a neat pile out of view. With a firm shake of my head, I pushed away the need to change the situation.

After another deep breath, I turned to face Max.

"Wow, Max, this is pretty great. Don't you think?"

"Absolutely." Max nodded as he glanced around. "Maybe Erik has a few good ideas up his sleeve after all."

I noticed a small booth set up not far from the cushions. It proclaimed itself a coffee shop. My first instinct was to get myself a cup of coffee, then I recalled what coffee shops often were in Amsterdam. It didn't take long for me to decipher that coffee was not always the main product being sold. Relax, Sammy, this is how it is here. It will only serve to open the minds of your fans anyway.

I tried to be cool and accept that mindset, but it was not how I really felt. I pictured myself reading to people with their mouths hanging open and their eyes fixated on the sky. That wasn't what I wanted to spend my time doing.

Just as I was about to point the coffee shop out to Max, Erik waved to us from the other side of the garden. "I'll be right there!"

I took a deep breath of the fragrant air and willed myself to be more interested in the good things than in the things that set my nerves on edge. I did notice that there was no table for a book signing to take place. I assumed it would be similar to the last book signing involving the beanbag chairs.

Erik jogged over to us. Adorned in bright loose clothing, he greeted us with a warm smile. "So? What do you think? Not too bad of a surprise, hm?"

"It's pretty nice." I smiled. "I'm glad you thought of moving things outside. I think it will give us all a new perspective."

"I'm so glad that you're happy with it. I really wasn't sure if you would be—especially with the dancers."

"Dancers?" I glanced around again. "What dancers?"

"Oh, over there." Erik pointed to a group of men and women who appeared to only be wearing leaves and petals. Most of each one's body was exposed.

"Erik? Why?" I couldn't form any other words. My eyes widened and my heart pounded.

"It just brings nature to life a bit, don't you think? You should see them move. It's like a poem in a person." He laughed. "That should be a title of a book, shouldn't it? What do you think, Samantha? Your next book could be called *A Poem in a Person*?"

I couldn't respond. My mind focused in on what would happen if any of those leaves fell off the dancers.

"I don't think this is going to work."

Max put his hands on my shoulders.

I took a slow breath.

"You haven't even seen them dance yet." Erik frowned.

"Erik, this is unreasonable. They don't have anything to do with my book."

"Are you sure?" He sighed. "I really thought that you, of all people, would be able to see what I'm trying to accomplish with this."

"I'm sorry, all I see are very loose leaves on very naked people."

"Wow. I'm pretty disappointed." His entire expression faded into one of sorrow. "I really expected more from you, Samantha."

"More from me?" I stared at him. "What about what I expect from you? I thought you were going to provide me with a normal book signing today."

"No need to get upset." Erik pursed his lips. "Do you want to get a coffee with me?"

"No, I don't want any pot!" I nearly screamed in frustration. This drew the attention of several of the guests who'd arrived for the book signing.

"Sounds like she needs some." The comment drifted from the group of dancers.

"No, I don't!"

Max leaned close to me. "Sammy, people are watching. Try to keep your voice down."

"No, I won't. I don't care if I'm not mellow or chill enough. This is important to me. My fans matter to me. I don't want to treat them to a circus. I want to treat them to a day where I have the opportunity to show my gratitude for their support. Not all of this nonsense!"

"Wow, okay. Right now you're just really killing my positive vibes." Erik shook his head. "Look, if you want me to fire all the dancers, I will."

The word "fire" hit me in the gut. I looked back at the group. They weren't just nearly naked people in a ridiculous get-up. They were people who needed to earn money. Why else would they let Erik do something like that to them? They were there expecting payment for their time.

"No, don't fire them." I sighed. I held back the fact that it was him who I'd like to fire. "It's too late to change things now. Let's just get this over with."

"If that's the kind of attitude you have, then how can we ever have a good experience?" Erik met my eyes. "Maybe if you spent a little more time opening your mind, you'd have a little less reason to get so upset."

"Now that's enough." Max glared at him as he stepped up beside Erik. "There's a big difference between having an open mind and making ridiculous choices. Just because Samantha would like things to be a little bit more traditional, that doesn't mean that she's automatically wrong. If you spent a nanosecond not baked out of your mind, you might see that."

LILLIANNA BLAKE

CHAPTER 24

Warmth filled me in reaction to Max's coming to my defense. He didn't have to, and yet he did.

"I can see that what they say about you Americans is pretty true." Erik frowned. "I thought Samantha would be different, though. I really did. That's why I planned all of these wild things. Not because I'm baked out of my mind, Max, but because I was trying to honor the woman I thought I'd gotten to know through her books— someone who isn't afraid to take chances, who likes to see things from new perspectives, who always has some great new idea. Are you sure you don't have a ghostwriter?" He scratched his head. "Maybe a really good editor?"

The wind was knocked right out of me. This man who had apparently started out as one of my supporters had completely transformed. The question was, was it his fault or mine?

Sure there were plenty of things that he did that I didn't like. I would even go so far as to say that most people probably wouldn't like them. But did that mean I should judge him for it? After all, I had resolved to have an open mind, and yet I shot down just about every one of his ideas. If I tried a little harder to be accepting, maybe things wouldn't have devolved to this point.

I took a deep cleansing breath and then shook my head.

"I'm starving. I've been rushing around so much today I don't think I've had anything to eat. Erik, just forget what I said. Give me a chance to get my blood sugar where it should be and we can go from there."

"Let me get you some food." Max rubbed my arm. "I'm sure there's something great nearby."

"There really isn't time for that. I might have something in my purse." I dug through it.

There was a time not so long ago that I would have always had some kind of healthy snack in my purse to keep me from getting too hungry. If I didn't have a little snack, then when I did eat, I was likely to eat a whole lot more. I'd gotten out of that habit with travel because of all the security checks.

When I heard the crinkle of a paper bag I remembered the cookies that the man at the coffee house had given me earlier.

"Score!" I pulled out the bag and opened it. "Do you want some?" I offered the cookie to Max.

"No, you eat it. You need to fill up."

"Erik?"

"Sorry, just had more than my share of brownie." He

chuckled.

I bit into the cookie. It crumbled across my tongue. The chocolate chips melted in the heat of my mouth. Maybe it was because I was so hungry, but the cookie tasted better than anything I'd eaten in recent memory. I quickly devoured it and started on the second. It didn't even bother me that Max and Erik stood there watching.

By the time I polished off the second cookie, I felt much better.

"There's one more thing I should probably tell you." Erik took the empty paper bag from me.

"What is it?" I smiled. It was amazing how much more relaxed I felt after getting some food in my stomach.

"I've planned a grand exit for you. Well, it's part grand exit and part my gift to you for being so open to my ideas. Obviously, I planned it before our little run-in. So if you want me to cancel it, I will. Just let me know."

"How can I know if you don't tell me?" I giggled.

Max looked over at me with a raised eyebrow.

"It's over there." Erik pointed across the park.

I saw it then—a huge orange hot-air balloon. I expected to be afraid. But instead I was quite thrilled.

"Wonderful. What an amazing idea. What a thoughtful gift." I stared into his eyes. "Erik, this might sound strange, but can I give you a hug?"

"Sammy?" Max moved toward me, but Erik opened his eyes wide.

"Bring it in—right here, Samantha! I knew that we'd get to be best friends after all this."

I settled into his arms and hugged him as tight as I could. He smelled good. His body gave out the most intense body heat. I wasn't aware that I rubbed my cheek against his chest until Max gave me a firm tap on the shoulder.

"Sammy? Are you feeling alright?"

"Yes." I sighed and pulled away from Erik. "I feel great. Let's get this book signing started!"

Max tried to catch my hand but I began to run across the grass toward the area where the cushions were set up. I had no idea why I had been so upset about them in the first place. I jumped from one to the other. With the force of each leap the wind blew through my hair. I was aware of Max calling out to me, but I ignored him. When I reached my cushion I plopped down with a laugh.

"Bring on the fans! I'm ready to blow this book signing out of the water!" I looked over at the dancers. "Well? What are you waiting for?"

Erik grinned. "I knew you'd come around." He hit a button on a hidden radio and music began to play.

CHAPTER 25

As the attendants of the book signing showed up one by one, the dancers weaved throughout them. A few people gave them a look, but most seemed rather impressed.

As the music tickled my senses, I began to move to the sound of it. My feet tapped. My arms rose up in the air above my head. I imagined myself swaying like a reed in shallow water. Soon all of my guests were doing the same. I realized that they thought it was part of the book signing. I saw no reason not to go with it.

I stood up and began to sway right along with the dancers. So did everyone around me. Soon we had our own little parade making our way around the entire park. As we danced, some were inspired to shed their clothes. I thought about it, but it seemed like a bit too much work to me.

People twirled, leaped, and even put lyrics to the music as the dancers weaved among us. When there was a lull in the music, people began to return to their cushions.

I became aware of Max very close to me just before he spoke in my ear.

"What exactly is that?" He jabbed a finger in the direction of a nearby man.

"Human, male." I raised an eyebrow. "Do you see something else, Max? A bicycle perhaps?" I giggled wildly.

"That is not funny." He pursed his lips and then pointed to the man again. "What is that on his chest?"

"Oh." My voice dropped as I noticed my signature on the man's chest. I had nearly forgotten about that odd autograph. "Relax, Max, it's just pen. It will wash off with time."

"Are you sure?" Max narrowed his eyes. "How did it get there?"

I poked him in the chest. "Are you jealous, Max?"

"Should I be? I mean, there's only a few ways that you could have signed his chest."

"He didn't have paper. I felt bad for the young lad." I giggled. "I'm trying an Irish accent, can you tell?"

"What? Why?" He shook his head, then looked at me with narrowed eyes. "What's going on with you?"

"Hey, I'm the one with my name on someone else's chest. I'm the one that should be asking the questions here."

"Sammy, what are you talking about?" Max's voice was strained. "You're not making any sense."

"Max, you worry too much. I'll show you." I waved to the man whose chest I'd signed. "You there. Yes, you.

Can you come over here for a minute?"

"Sammy, that's not necessary."

"Sure it is. I want you to feel comfortable, Max. See, it's just pen." I licked my thumb and began to scrub it across the man's chest.

"Careful there." He drew back from my touch. "The ink's still wet." He grinned at me.

"How can that be? It's been a while since I signed you."

"Oh no, not that kind of ink. Tattoo ink." He pointed to the signature. "It's permanent."

"Why?" I stared at him with wide eyes.

"I have a bit of a crush on Zara." He shrugged. "I figured this was the closest I could get to her. The artist did a good job, didn't he?"

"Yes." I trailed my fingertips lightly along the raised surface. "It looks just like my signature."

"Sammy, maybe we should get back to the book signing." Max pulled me back from the man as he stared at him intently. "And *you* should put your shirt back on."

I noticed that his tone had become a bit gruff.

"Max, relax, please. It's always wonderful to have a fan."

"I hear you, but it's a little odd for a fan to be that fanatic, don't you think?"

"Are you just jealous because he got my name tattooed on him before you could?" I winked at him.

He tilted his head to the side and looked me over

slowly. "Have you been drinking?"

"I'm not going to answer that." I giggled and plopped back down on my cushion.

As the dancers finally settled down, so did the rest of the guests. I breathed a sigh of relief when everyone was finally seated. All of the whirling and twirling had inspired a wave of dizziness that I couldn't seem to shake.

As I sat before the group, a strong desire arose within me to not just share a piece of my book with them, but a piece of me. I began reading the passage I'd chosen from *Becoming Zara*. As I finished the words, I looked out at the audience. Each person appeared enthralled, but were they really? I wasn't so sure.

I sat up and drew my knees up to my chest.

"I'd like to get real with you here now. Nothing too heavy, I promise. But I'd like to talk about how easy it is to turn a good thing into a bad thing. Or sometimes, to not give something a chance to be anything at all.

"It is far too easy to get stressed and automatically react to an unfamiliar situation. The rush to judgment is a hard thing to fight. We've perhaps had an experience in the past that triggers a flood of emotions regarding what is happening now. That flood of emotions threatens to send us into a panic if we're not careful. As the wheels begin to turn in our flight or fight response we lose sight of a perfect opportunity—a chance to embrace the unknown, the unpredictable. What if, instead of an automatic negative response, we entertained the idea before us? What if we chose to explore it to see where it led?

"Many times we've been trained into a pattern of thought. Either our parents, our teachers, or life experiences have taught us that certain things are off limits or far too risky. However, as we explore life, it's easy to see that every single experience is very different. Once we see that, we begin to recognize that, even though our hesitation might be founded, that doesn't mean that it is valid. One step in what we perceive as the wrong direction could truly lead us to something beautiful."

I stopped to finally get a breath, noting the confusion on some of the faces before me, but also the nodding of heads. "I know, I preach trusting your instincts all the time. But, the question to ask yourself is whether the reaction is your genuine instinct or an instinct that you've been taught. Each decision will be different, each experience will be different, but living a life of automatic 'no's can rob us of multitudes of experiences.

"Think about times that you've backed out of an activity out of fear or self-consciousness. How might things have been different with a bit more boldness? It's pretty easy to assume that nothing good will come out of taking a risk; however, the truth is that most of the world's great inventions, fantastic art, and groundbreaking discoveries were a result of a very risky choice."

I cleared my throat. "I'm not advocating putting

yourself in dangerous situations. I just think it might be worth pausing for a moment before automatically denying yourself an experience."

CHAPTER 26

A round of applause rose throughout the crowd. Each steady slap of palm against palm startled me a little. It was such a harsh noise. How had I not noticed it before?

For an instant, I thought of the entire crowd as a herd of seals flapping their fins together. It was such a funny thought that I began to laugh.

The more I laughed, the more intense my dizziness became. I couldn't focus on the crowd anymore. They'd become a distant blur.

"Samantha." Erik hissed in my ear. "Time to wrap it up."

Wrap it up, I thought. Make the world stop spinning. I blinked a few times and my vision cleared.

"Thanks, everyone! You've been great! I really feel like I've connected with each of you on a really deep level." I took a deep breath and then sighed. "What a beautiful day. What a beautiful experience. You're all so very beautiful."

The entire audience burst into applause as I stood up.

Bolstered by their admiration, I became certain that I would make the perfect next president of the United States—or maybe the next Queen of England. I was headed to London, after all. I wondered if I could become a queen or if I had to be born into it. Being president seemed a bit easier.

I stood up and gave a presidential wave to my audience.

Erik leaned close. "Are you ready for your grand exit?"

"Yes—yes, I am." I grinned and held onto his elbow as he led me to the hot air balloon. The world seemed to be swaying a bit under my feet.

Erik tightened his grip on me. "Samantha, are you okay? Are you sick?"

"I'm fine." I laughed. "Aren't you fine? I'm sure you are. We're all fine."

"Are you sure that you're up for this, Samantha?"

"Of course I am. Up, you know—like the balloon goes up, up in the air." I grinned at him. "I can't wait!"

"Okay." He looked over his shoulder. "Where's Max? Don't you want him to go with you?"

"Never mind about Max. He's so cranky today. I'm ready to fly! Set me free, Erik!" I waved my hands in the air and rocked the hot air balloon back and forth.

"Alright, just be careful. I'll get the pilot, he'll join you for the ride."

"A pilot?" I frowned as Erik walked away.

The last thing I wanted to do was be stuck on a hot air balloon with a stranger. Instead, I decided that I was going to take flight all on my own. I needed to be more focused on myself, not on what weighed me down. I reached for the cord that anchored the hot air balloon. I wasn't sure what I was doing exactly, but I did know that it needed to be done.

With a hard swift tug I freed the rope from its anchor. A moment later, the hot air balloon began to rise. Below me I saw people leaving the book signing and I saw Max near the entrance of the park.

Then I saw Erik running and screaming. He didn't look mellow at all. I laughed and waved to him as the hot air balloon drifted.

There were some trees ahead. It occurred to me that I had no idea how to make the hot air balloon go higher or lower. I remembered something from a movie about cords and fire, but I had no idea which to pull. I shrugged and decided to just let things flow.

When I looked back down at the ground again there was a huge crowd of people under me. They were all shouting and waving their hands at me.

I narrowed my eyes. "What are you all screaming about?" I shook my head. "It's beautiful up here." I looked back at the sky in time to see the tree line that was quickly approaching.

My heartbeat quickened. The trees. What was going

to happen when I hit the trees? I couldn't wrap my head around what I should do.

I looked back down at the ground again. To my surprise there was Max. It surprised me even more to see him on a bicycle. He seemed to be pedaling so fast that I thought he might end up flying.

"Oh, Max! I'm so proud of you!" I waved to him from the basket. "Look at you! You're doing so good! You're so amazing!"

Max pedaled even faster.

In the distance I heard a siren. I looked back at the sky. But all I saw was trees.

"Oh no." It finally hit me that I was in quite a bit of danger. All of a sudden the hot air balloon slowed its progress.

I looked down to see that Max, now off the bike, had the rope wrapped around his hands. The balloon was so strong that it was pulling him across the ground. But the more he tugged, the lower and slower the balloon moved.

Soon other people gathered around him to pull on the rope and the balloon eased much closer to the ground.

"Okay, I've had enough." I tossed one leg over the side of the balloon basket.

"Wait!" Max shouted. "I think you're still a bit high to jump, Sammy!"

"I'll be fine! Don't worry so much!" I laughed and swung the other leg outside of the basket.

"Samantha, no!" Max held up his hands.

"Yes, Max! Catch me!" I flung myself out of the basket.

In my mind I was a swan leaping into my lover's arms. In reality, I plastered Max against the ground amidst shrieks from onlookers.

I gazed into his eyes and smiled.

CHAPTER 27

"Sammy. Where did you get those cookies?" Max smiled back at me, but he sounded more than slightly out of breath.

The question struck me as funny, so I giggled. I laughed so hard that I rolled off him and stretched out in the grass. Above me the sky glistened with shards of sunlight.

"So beautiful."

Max shook his head. "Maybe we need to get you to a doctor."

"No, Max. The sky is healing me. Here, see for yourself." I patted the grass beside me.

Around us people rushed to pin down the hot air balloon. But I barely noticed. The sky swallowed me whole and rocked me in its wispy clouds. Max stretched out beside me. His elbow brushed against mine; the crease of his sleeve tickled the tender skin. I laughed again and stretched my arms out beside me.

"Isn't life magical, Max?" I looked over at him.

Max smiled at me. He didn't point out that I'd

squashed him, or that he had to race to catch up with me, or even that those cookies were likely spiked. He just stared into my eyes and smiled.

"You make it magical, Sammy—every single day."

I grinned and rolled over to kiss him. As the chaos dwindled around us, I lost myself in Max's warm lips and loving arms. There, once more, I relaxed. Not because of the cookies, but because of his acceptance and the unconditional love that he showed me.

He looked into my eyes and smiled. "What are you thinking right now?"

"Honestly?" I studied him in return.

"Yes. Honestly."

"I'm starving."

"Ah, yes—the munchies." He laughed. "Let's get you to the nearest restaurant." He escorted me out of the park.

I didn't even notice the strange looks that I knew were being directed at me. It wasn't until we reached the exit of the park that I even remembered there were other people in the world aside from Max—and this was only because of the angry man that charged up to us.

"You stole my bike! I saw you do it. Don't even try to deny it."

His voice sounded so familiar, not because I'd met him before, but because it was the same tone I'd used with Erik earlier in the day. The thought that I could be that wound up and stressed out horrified me all of a sudden.

Max frowned. "I borrowed it. I didn't steal it. It's right where I left it at the center of the park. I needed it to save my wife."

"I don't care why you needed it, it wasn't yours to take. If I find a scratch on it, you will buy me a new one."

"That's fine. Here." Max reached into his wallet and handed him a business card. "This is where you can reach me. Just let me know if your bike needs any repairs."

"Plan on hearing from me." He glared at Max.

Max guided me past him and out of the park.

About twenty minutes later, with my mouth stuffed to the brim, it hit me all at once. I blinked. Then the subtle relaxation that filled me disappeared. One by one the events of the day paraded through my mind. The dance that the peculiar thoughts did inside my head taunted me.

"Max, oh my God. Max, what did I do?"

He pushed another container of cheesy fries toward me. "Don't worry about it now, Sammy."

Worry. The word slammed into me like a truck. I'd spent about three hours not worrying about anything. All at once all of my concerns had returned, heavier than ever.

I recalled my not-so-graceful landing.

"Max, did I hurt you?" I looked into his eyes.

"No, I'm fine." He took my hand in his. "It's not your fault, so don't even go there."

"Sure it is."

"No, it's not. You ate some spiked cookies and—well, stole a hot air balloon."

"Am I going to jail?" I grimaced.

"No jail for you." He patted my hand. "You just need a little time to recover."

"Wait." I wracked my mind, then looked back at him. "Was I hallucinating or were you riding a bike?"

"Yes, I was. I needed to get to you fast, and there was one close to me."

"So I stole a hot air balloon and you stole a bike." I laughed. "We're both going to jail."

"Stop saying that before you give someone an idea." He grinned. "It was quite an adventure."

"I'm so proud of you for overcoming your fear, Max."

"Thank you, Sammy. But I only did it because you were in trouble. I didn't think twice about it."

"It's interesting that you say that. I'm sure that my inhibitions were reduced by the pot, and even though it led to some questionable choices, I have to say I learned something from it."

"What?" Max searched my eyes. "How not to get off a hot air balloon?"

"No." I winked at him. "I learned what it feels like to be free of all my worry—of my need for control."

"A little more control would have helped in that situation."

"You're absolutely right. But I did enjoy that sensation of freedom. I want to experience that more in my life. I'm always trying to control things that are either out of my control or don't really need to be controlled. It's time I started practicing a little more relaxing and a little less stressing."

"Here's to that." Max held up his glass of soda.

I clinked it with my glass of water. It was a perfect ending to a groundbreaking day. Although the cookies had been a mistake, I didn't regret it. I'd learned a lesson I might not have learned otherwise.

There was one more person I needed to thank. The one man I thought would ruin my trip to Amsterdam had proven to open my mind in very unexpected ways.

On the walk back to the shipping container, I recalled the way it felt to look into the sky. It made me feel free— that there was no beginning and no end. Perhaps that was the lack of control that I needed.

As it was now, I saw things with a beginning and an end. Maybe I needed to embrace the concept of infinity.

CHAPTER 28

When we returned to the shipping container, Erik
greeted us at the door.

"I thought you two might prefer a hotel tonight. I
realize that I may have driven you two a little too much in
the wrong direction." He frowned and looked over at me.
"I'm sorry, Samantha—about the book signing, about the
shipping container, about everything."

"Oh, please. Don't be." I smiled and patted his cheek.
"You shouldn't be sorry about any of that. You've made
me very happy."

Erik stared at me for a moment, then he looked past
me at Max. "She's still high, isn't she?"

"No, I don't think so." Max laughed. "She's turned
over a new leaf."

"Really?" Erik studied me. "Just what was in those
cookies?"

"I'm not exactly sure, but whatever it was, I don't
need to experience it again. The book signings were
perfect. I really hope that you believe me. I don't think
there will be any that are more memorable than this last

one."

"Ah, just wait until you have your meeting with Poppy. She flew in to meet with you this evening before you head off to London."

"Wow, I feel like we just got here." Max rubbed his head.

"We did just get here." I met his eyes. "That's the life of being on tour."

"I wouldn't trade it." He kissed my forehead. "I just hope we get some down time in London. I'm ready for a little rest after this wild ride."

"Is that a dig?" Erik smirked. "Because I feel like it's a dig."

"I think Max is referring to the bath in the canal."

"That, or the tablet to the nose, or the leap off the hot air balloon." Max rubbed his neck. "I'm pretty sure I'm going to need a massage."

"I can help you with that." I smiled and rubbed his shoulders.

"Well, before you two get started on that, here is your hotel key and this is the restaurant where Poppy will meet you for brunch tomorrow. Don't be late. She hates it when people are late."

"Hm. It sounds like we might get along."

"Ha-ha." Erik winked at me. "Just remember, when you want to come back to Amsterdam and have the best time of your life, there's only one name to speak."

"Yes, what was the name of that coffee shop owner?"

"Now you're funny? I spent all this time trying to get you to loosen up and now you joke around?"

"Oh, she's funny, trust me." Max grinned.

"When I visit again, we'll spend some time getting to know one another, Erik. I think there's a lot more you could teach me about living a mellow lifestyle."

"And I'm sure there's some perks to your desire for organization." He shrugged. "Maybe."

"Thanks again, Erik."

"Any time."

As Erik walked away, Max nudged me with his shoulder. "Are you coming back to Amsterdam for Erik or the cookies?"

"Maybe a little of both." I winked at him.

The hotel room appeared vast in comparison to the shipping container we'd been staying in—the bed embarrassingly luxurious. I flopped down on it and yawned. With one finger I poked my belly.

"I think I ate too much. I made up for all my attempts to diet since I've been on tour."

Max stretched out beside me and pushed up my shirt. "Looks good to me." He grinned and then planted several kisses along my stomach.

"Stop! You're tickling me!" I laughed and pushed him away. "I love you, Max."

"I know. Even if you've tried to kill me a few times, I still know that you love me."

"I didn't try to kill you."

"No, you didn't succeed." He wrapped his arms around me and yawned against my shoulder. "But you definitely tried."

"Max, don't say that." I passed my hand back through his hair. "I got you back on the bike, didn't I?"

"Oh, you're going to take credit for that?" He laughed, then looked into my eyes. "It's true, you did. When I saw you floating away in the hot air balloon, all I could think about was getting you back. I didn't even hesitate. You have that much power over me, Sammy."

"Just remember that the next time we end up in a canal."

"Next time?" He smiled slyly. "Next time we'll have to find Erik's old swimming hole."

I fell asleep with a smile on my face, and strange thoughts about cookies and swimming holes floating through my mind.

When I woke the next morning, Max still slept soundly next to me. I brushed a few kisses along his cheek, then eased my way out of bed. It was much simpler than trying to climb over him. I didn't even get tangled up in the blanket.

I was quite curious about meeting Poppy. London was a mystery to me. Despite the fact that it had the least of a language barrier, I wondered if I would fit in with the culture. On one hand it could be very eccentric, and on the other it could be very proper.

While I showered, I tried to figure out what would be best to wear. I decided to go slightly casual, selecting a brightly colored blouse and simple slacks.

I spent a little time on my make-up—more than I usually did. After the incident the day before, I had a few blemishes to cover up.

Once I'd finished I looked over to see that Max was still asleep. He'd had quite an adventurous day too. I scribbled a note for him and placed it on the bedside table.

On my way out the door I grabbed my purse and a notebook. I hoped that the woman I was meeting would be a little more organized than Erik had been.

CHAPTER 29

The cab ride to the restaurant was fairly short. When I arrived, the restaurant was nearly empty.

"Excuse me?" I looked at the hostess. "I'm supposed to be meeting someone."

"I have a table reserved under Poppy Cantwell. Is that who you are meeting?"

"Yes." I smiled.

"She's not here yet, but I can seat you."

"Great. Thank you so much." I followed her to a small table.

"Would you like to order?"

"No, I'll wait. I'll just have a water, please."

"I'll be back with it in a minute."

"Thanks."

A minute later, just as she'd promised, she returned with the water. I toyed with the straw in the glass. With every second I waited I became a little more insecure. Was she coming at all? Would she be a no-show like Erik had been at first?

I stroked my fingers through my hair and smoothed it

down. My mind was still swimming with the memories of the day before. It wasn't exactly that I regretted it, but being that out of control was a brand new experience for me.

I shifted in my chair and glanced at my watch again—ten minutes past the time of the meeting. I double-checked my phone to be sure that the name of the restaurant was correct.

When I looked up from my phone, I saw a woman strolling toward me. She wore a neat, snug pantsuit with wide lapels that reminded of a few decades before. Her dark hair was wound into a smooth bun at the top of her head. Every step she took was produced with even grace and determination.

I smiled at her, anticipating a smile in return.

Instead, she paused, looked me over, then sat down in the chair across from me. "Samantha."

"Yes, I'm Samantha."

"I know that." She cleared her throat and placed her phone in the middle of the table. "I'm Poppy. I will be your contact in England. I thought perhaps visiting you here would give us a chance to get to know one another. However, I don't need to try very hard to get to know you, do I, Samantha?"

I stared at her. The cool tone of her voice made me think there was a serious problem.

"What do you mean?" I smiled a little. "Because you're a fan of my book?"

"I'm not sure that I can say that. I have read it. I did enjoy it. But I expected a lot more from you." She clucked her tongue and shook her head.

"I have to say that I'm confused by what you're saying. Have we met before? Maybe I don't recall?" I narrowed my eyes. She didn't look familiar to me, and I thought I would have remembered those striking brown eyes and the lilt of her English accent.

"No, unfortunately we haven't met before. I do wish that we would have. Perhaps, if we'd met before this, I'd have more of an idea of who you really are to combat what I've been forced to see here." She tapped her phone screen.

Before I could question her further, I saw the screen come to life with a video. To my horror, it was me waving to Max from the hot air balloon and begging for him to catch me.

"Where did you get that?" I looked up at her with wide eyes.

"It doesn't matter where. What matters is that I could have gotten it from any number of sources. It's all over the Internet right now, and it's not likely that it will fade away any time soon. In it you're clearly impaired. Aren't you?"

I swallowed hard. It was a conversation I never expected to have. I didn't normally take chances that led to uncomfortable discussions like this.

"I was, but I wasn't even aware that I was."

"What does that even mean?" She frowned. "I know here in Amsterdam things are different, but you need to understand that I offered my book shop to you out of support of your inspirational book—because I thought it bolstered the role of women in literature. But this shows me the complete opposite."

"Wait, please. You have the wrong idea."

"Videos don't lie, Samantha."

"No, they don't." I sighed. "But I don't want you to have the wrong impression of me. If you'll just hear me out, I'll be able to explain everything."

"Shall we order first?" She waved her hand in the air.

Three waitresses rushed over.

I raised an eyebrow. The woman certainly had a commanding presence.

One waitress lingered beside the table. "What can I get for you ladies?"

I was very aware that the video was still playing on the phone. I reached out to try to block it. "I'll just have a salad—and some water."

"I'll take the steak and the side of rice without any excessive butter. Please."

"Coming right up." The waitress walked away.

I looked across the table at Poppy.

"The truth is, I ate a special cookie without knowing what was inside. I was aware of what I was doing, but I couldn't stop myself from doing it. It was an honest mistake."

"And conveniently made in Amsterdam?" She shook her head. "It doesn't matter now, but I want to warn you, my book shop is a sacred place for me and my circle of friends. I don't want it disrespected."

"I can assure you that I won't do anything of the kind. I'm looking forward to visiting London and your shop."

"Are you?"

She met my eyes with a quiet intensity that left me a little rattled inside. It seemed to me that how I answered the question would decide the direction our relationship took.

"Yes, I am." I leaned forward some. "Poppy, I didn't mean to create this wild situation and certainly didn't expect it to be recorded for everyone to see on the Internet. But I have to tell you, I don't regret it."

"You don't regret getting high and causing an emergency situation?" She arched an eyebrow and pursed her lips. "That doesn't make sense to me."

"I do regret causing anyone any trouble, but I don't regret discovering that I was bound by some seriously heavy need for control. It limited me to such an extreme that I couldn't even enjoy the fact that my book is doing well. Instead of finding ways to celebrate while on tour, I've been looking for reasons that I might fail. A short amount of time without those fears did wonders for my perspective."

"Be that as it may, the method you used is not

acceptable, at least not in London."

"I agree. I am never one to partake of that kind of activity. Like I said, I made a mistake. I didn't realize the cookies I ate were marijuana cookies. What happened as a result still can be a benefit for me, instead of my hiding out somewhere to avoid embarrassment."

She nodded. "I like that you're willing to find something positive to take from the situation, but the fact remains that my expectations of you are shaken. I want to be certain that my customers are treated correctly. I won't have any tomfoolery in my shop."

CHAPTER 30

I studied Poppy for a moment. She appeared to be my age, but the rigid way she carried herself reminded me of someone much older.

"Do you have a plan for the book signings?"

"Itemized." She reached down into her soft-sided briefcase and pulled out a thick folder. "I've got every minute of your stay in London planned."

"Oh. Usually there's a day for my husband and me to explore."

"You'll be exploring, under the supervision of a tour guide. I can't risk you getting hurt, lost, or otherwise detained." She quirked a brow. "Especially with that in your system."

I gritted my teeth. The woman seems to be doing her best to make me feel like a criminal. "We're capable of keeping ourselves out of trouble."

She pointed to her phone again. "Not according to that video."

"Poppy, it was a mistake."

"I can't afford mistakes, Samantha. I built this business with my own hands from the ground up. I support my daughter with this business and I will not have it harmed by some silly antics of a woman who still thinks that she's a girl."

I was taken aback by the hostility in her tone. "Poppy, I would never do anything to threaten the well-being of your business. I think we've gotten off on the wrong foot here."

"Don't worry about your feet, Samantha. Just make sure that when you arrive in London, you're prepared to get to know more fans than you've likely met on the tour. *Becoming Zara* is very popular in London and the books are flying off the shelves."

"That's great news."

"It is." She smiled a little. "And—I have read it. I am a fan, Samantha."

"Oh, good." I laughed. "I was starting to worry there for a minute."

"You should be worried." She locked eyes with me. "Just because I'm a fan, that doesn't mean that I will do anything to risk my business. It was nice meeting you, Samantha." She stood up from the table and offered me her hand.

"Aren't you going to eat?" I took her hand in a quick shake.

"I can't. I have another appointment. We'll talk in London."

"Okay. Thanks!" I smiled at her, but she'd already turned toward the door.

I ordered some food for Max and me to share at the hotel, then headed back to meet him.

When I entered the hotel room, it looked as if he'd just woken up. The sheet was crumpled and I could hear the shower on full blast. I made us a picnic in our enormous bed and wondered what surprises London had in store for us.

As nervous as Erik's loose attitude had made me, Poppy seemed so rigid that she might just snap. If things went as awry in London as they had in Amsterdam, she would snap right before my eyes.

Max stepped out of the bathroom with a towel around his waist and a mop of wet hair. "Back early?"

"I brought brunch to you." I smiled.

He held my gaze. "What's wrong?"

"Get out of my head, Max." I laughed.

He hopped into the bed and snuggled close to me. I ignored the fact that his hair was dripping water all over me.

"Honesty, remember?"

I sighed. "London may be interesting. I'm just a little nervous."

"As always." He kissed me lightly then began to dig into his brunch. "It will all work out, Sammy. Doesn't it always?"

"As long as I'm with you, Max." I grinned. "Whatever

happens in London, will happen. But if we're together, it'll all be just fine."

"Speaking of being together. I have a friend in London that I'd like you to meet."

"A friend? Does he live in London?"

"Yes, she does—and she's looking forward to our visit."

I thought about the tight schedule that Poppy had suggested we'd have. "I'm sure we can find a way to fit it in."

"Great."

Max devoured the remainder of his brunch, but my appetite had faded.

I was certain that London would be full of surprises, and all the cookies in Amsterdam couldn't make me like surprises.

A NOTE FROM THE AUTHOR

Fictional character, Samantha Bradford and the Single Wide Female books are written for every woman out there who has struggled with their weight, self-esteem and any number of issues that we all face as we work to become the best versions of ourselves that we can be.

These books are meant to be light-hearted and fun, with the hope that they will also inspire you to make your own "bucket list" of sorts—and to REALLY live your life to the fullest, loving yourself completely as you do so.

Lillianna loves to hear from her readers and can be contacted via her website where you can also download a complimentary book.

LilliannaBlake.com

ALL TITLES BY LILLIANNA BLAKE

http://Amazon.com/author/lilliannablake
*Check the author page for current list of titles

Single Wide Female: The Bucket List
#1 Learn Pole Dancing
#2 Start a Blog
#3 Learn to Cook
#4 Create a Masterpiece
#5 Run a Marathon
#6 Go Skinny Dipping
#7 Start Online Dating
#8 Learn Yoga
#9 Be a Mentor
#10 Crash a Wedding
#11 Be a Movie Extra
#12 Join a Writing Group
#13 Enjoy a Spa Day
#14 Donate Blood
#15 Learn Poker
#16 Get a Tattoo
#17 Host a Dinner Party
#18 Publish a Book
#19 Walk Across Hot Coals
#20 Learn to Swim
#21 Learn to Meditate
#22 Quit My Job
#23 Learn to Salsa
#24 Fall in Love

Single Wide Female in Love
#1 The Date
#2 The Girlfriend
#3 The Fiancée
#4 The Wife

Single Wide Female Travels
#1 Sammy in France
#2 Sammy in Italy
#3 Sammy in Holland
#4 Sammy in England

Other Single Wide Female Titles
My Valentine's Day
St. Paddy's Day Disaster
A Bunny Tale
Sammy's Christmas List

Becoming Zara
*how the B.I.G. Girls Club came to be

B.I.G. Girls Club
The Rockstar's Girlfriend
The Former Model

Visit the author website at LilliannaBlake.com to get on the notification list for new releases and to receive a complimentary book to learn what inspired Sammy to begin her bucket list.